UNIDENTIFIED

MIKEL J. WISLER

SCIENCE FICTION MEETS SOCRATES

UNIDENTIFIED

MIKEL J. WISLER

Published by DoxaNoûs Media
Marion, Indiana 46952—www.doxanousmedia.com

Based on the screenplay by the same title, also by Mikel J. Wisler.

Cover design: Mikel J. Wisler
Interior layout: Mikel J. Wisler
Editor: Eric M. Bumpus

Printed in the United States of America

ISBN: 978-1-7325307-6-8 (pbk)   ISBN: 978-1-7325307-7-5 (ebk)

For information about the author, visit: www.mikelwisler.com

Second Edition: January 2020
10 9 8 7 6 5 4 3 2 1

Type Face: the text of this book is printed using EB Garamond
Copyright © 2010, 2011 Georg Duffner (http://www.georgduffner.at)
EB Garamond is licensed under the SIL Open Font License, Version 1.1.

Title and chapter title font: Gesso, freeware typeface by Ryoichi Tsunekawa, Flat-it: http://flat-it.com.

Back cover font: Raleway, Copyright © 2010 - 2012, Matt McInerney, Pablo Impallari, Rodrigo Fuenzalida, with Reserved Font Name "Raleway". Raleway is licensed under the SIL Open Font License, Version 1.1.

FOR KSK

WE HAD A GOOD RUN... TILL WE DIDN'T.

COMING IN 2021
FIVE PART FULL CAST AUDIO DRAMA

ACKNOWLEDGEMENTS

IN THE PROCESS OF writing this novel and screenplay (which happened in tandem), I relied heavily on the help of many people. First and foremost, I thank my wife, Danae, without whom none of the storytelling I do would be possible. My thanks to Jedidiah Burdick who helped light a fire in my imagination for making this not just a feature film script, but a novel as well. Thank you to Eric Bumpus and Tom Conners, who read the early drafts of the novel and gave me valuable feedback. Thank you also to Dominic and Kristina Stone Kaiser. Both of them have provided such invaluable input, feedback, thoughtful questions, and encouragement as they read everything from a very rough and naked early outline to the finished screenplay and novel.

My thanks to Trevor Duke, who though not a fan of the horror genre, allowed me the incredibly enlightening experience of telling him my whole outline for this story over beers one night. He's even shot interviews with me for our early marketing materials. Thank you you also to Luana Bessa for reading this novel and providing me with specific feedback as it relates to the fields of therapy and psychiatry as well as to James Ross Otis for giving me feedback in relation to military deployment. I must extend a big thank you to the editor of this manuscript, Jeremiah Hawn. Your keen eye and insightful suggestions will make me come across as a far better writer than I am. Thank you Eric Bumpus again for helping me with the Kindle formatting and the publishing process and constant encouragement.

A big thank you to Kate Paulsen, the woman on the cover of this book, who read the screenplay and agreed to dive in with both feet into being part of this project as the model for the cover art and the lead actress as soon as we can secure the funding for the feature film. Along those lines, thank you also to Rajah Samaroo for the feedback on the script and all the support and enthusiasm for this project and willingness to sign on so early in development as the cinematographer for the film. Thank you both for taking such a big risk on me!

My thanks also to the people of Lincoln and North Woodstock, New Hampshire. I have visited multiple times and have always found the people warm and welcoming and the towns and scenery absolutely lovely. I have taken many liberties in fictionalizing versions of both towns in this story that are dealing with on-going cases of UFO sightings and abductions. To my knowledge, no one in these real towns has been abducted by aliens.

Finally, in writing this novel, I drew heavily upon the research compiled in the book, *UFO's: A Scientific Debate* edited by Carl Sagan and Thornton Page.

Man has traditionally tended to construct a myth to explain anything he cannot understand. And this is precisely the way that flying saucers or UFO's came into existence.

- Donald H. Menzel,

UFO's — The Modern Myth

When Galileo's telescope made it possible to sight the moons of Jupiter, many refused to look through the telescope. They "knew" that there could not be such bodies around Jupiter, and therefore they "knew" that the telescope was a deceptive instrument.

- Robert L. Hall,

Sociological Perspectives on UFO Reports

Science began as an outgrowth for theology, and all scientists, whether atheists or theists ... accept an essentially theological worldview.

- Paul Davies,

Are We Alone?: Philosophical Implications of the Discovery of Extraterrestrial Life

There is a wide range of concepts which would be fascinating especially if only they were true. But precisely because these ideas have charm, exactly because they are of deep emotional significance to us, they are the ideas we must examine most critically. We must consider them with the greatest skepticism, and examine in the greatest detail the evidence relevant to them. Where we have an emotional stake in an idea, we are most likely to deceive ourselves.

- Carl Sagan,

UFO's: The Extraterrestrial and Other Hypotheses

INTRODUCTION

There is a hush that surrounds these things. A seemingly impenetrable invisible wall of silence wraps certain mysteries in life. Overwhelmed by the unknown—or is it the perverse nature of such events?—words fail most people. The temptation to move forward and carry on with daily life as if such things were not a reality is quite strong. This seems an understandable response in the first world, dominated by lives quietly—and most often unknowingly—shaped by materialism and empiricism. That which can be owned becomes the real focus. That which we believe is accepted through mainstream general consensus of the collected evidence of our age.

So it was in early 2011 when a collection of startling and unsettling events took place in and around the town of North Woodstock, New Hampshire. This small town, just southwest of Lincoln, was known for its brewery and shops as far as most tourists are concerned. The town, which mostly consists of businesses stretching down Main Street, has a few surrounding houses in a small neighborhood. Most of the rest of the town's inhabitants live in the surrounding area within the town limits. From the center of town the tree-covered peaks of the surrounding mountains can be seen in every direction. It's a quiet place with kind people. But a rash of odd experiences had become the talk of the town for several years. Lights had been spotted in the skies several times, nearby livestock had been found mutilated overnight, several people reported seeing strange persons or beings on their property, others heard noises or could not account for hours of a given evening.

The following year, Jeffery Bines, a bit of a local recluse who occasionally ventured into town to buy a few things at the Fadden General Store or enjoy some drinks at Truant's Tavern or the brewery, was found walking down main street one night nude and incoherent. Local police took him in for the night. Bines claimed he had no idea how he had ended up in town. His truck was found on his property six miles south of town. Bines explained that three nights before, he'd seen lights hovering in the sky over the trees on his property. Since that night, he'd been waking up in strange places in various states of undress. He was unable to recall how he'd gotten to such places or what had transpired in the time since he'd gone to bed and the time he had come to.

The night he was arrested was the farthest from home he had ever found himself. Police placed little stock in his strange tale, however. Meanwhile, talk in the town continued to grow. Some were quick to dismiss his claims, while others wondered if anyone was safe. Two weeks later, Bines' ex-wife reported him missing after she hadn't managed to contact him on the phone for a week and thus went by his house only to find his truck and all his belongings exactly as they should have been aside from one small detail: his door was unlocked and ajar. Bines, a very private man, as a rule always locked up. It was as if Bines had simply gotten up one day and walked off into the surrounding woods. Certainly some in town attributed his disappearance to Bines' known affinity for hard liquor. Others, however, found renewed reason to believe Bines' original claims of contact with UFOs. In any case, he was never found.

Just as folks in the area were starting to move past such strangeness, however, new talk emerged of more UFO sightings in the area. It all came to a head when news was leaked that a local family claimed to have been experiencing alien abductions. Jim and Tammy Ferguson claimed psychiatric therapy had revealed that their son, Tommy, had been abducted multiple times. Naturally, skepticism prevailed until one night in April of 2014, Tommy vanished. An in-depth investigation that involved the cooperation of local police and the FBI followed. But in the months that followed Tommy's vanishing, little progress was made in ascertaining his whereabouts or confirming the allegations of alien abduction his parents continued to hold to so firmly. Ultimately, after a year of waiting, the Fergusons no longer found North Woodstock and the surrounding areas to be all that comforting of a place to live and moved away. Tommy's case remained technically open, but no one really believed there was any hope of a resolution, that is, until a new case emerged in town. Hushed whispers returned and suspicions were stirred again. Whatever one might think of such matters, one thing was clear: an invisible gloom seemed to hang over the area again, thick as fog.

CHAPTER ONE

HER SCAR HURT AGAIN, and this was always unsettling. Stephanie looked out of the car window at the nearly moonless night and tried to distract her mind, which seemed determined to fixate on the small scar on the back of her neck. Silvia, who drove the old Camry while talking with Annette, pulled over and stopped the car. Outside, the driveway to Stephanie's parents' house stretched away from the road, pine trees lined both sides. Normally, this was a welcomed sight, a comfort. But tonight, looking out that window, Stephanie felt as if the darkness appeared somehow more intensely black and the driveway longer and surrounded by unseen dangers.

"Are you sure you don't wanna' come?" Silvia looked back at Stephanie in the back seat. "Eddie will be there."

"I'm sure," Stephanie replied, not taking her eyes off the driveway.

"Well, look, the movie starts in ten minutes. We have to get to the theater in Lincoln. So ..." said Silvia, doing little to mask her annoyance.

"Thanks for the ride," Stephanie mumbled, and opened her door.

She exited the car and watched it pull away. How could she explain how she felt to them when she wasn't even sure how to rationally explain it to herself. She wished they would have told her ahead of time the evening's plan included going to the theater in Lincoln to watch a horror movie. She felt stupid for insisting on being dropped off at home instead of going with the rest of them. Maybe she should have forced herself to go, but she couldn't put herself through that, not anymore. It was hard enough to sleep most nights now as it was. She didn't need to infest her mind with even more nightmares, imagined or otherwise.

Turning, she began to walk down the gravel driveway that led up to the log cabin house her parents, Tim and Dorothy Clark, had owned for the past eleven years. A subtle pulsing sense emitted from the small scar on the back of Stephanie's neck. It sat right over her spine and most days, it was something she thought little of. It had randomly appeared there almost a year ago, but she had no recollection of what had caused it in the first place. But one thing seemed certain, any time it bothered her, she had a bad night.

As she made her way up the driveway, an increasingly familiar feeling crept over her body. Her skin crawled, and a chill traveled through her in spite of the warm summer night. She was being watched, she was sure of it. Try as she may to keep her eyes locked on the house up ahead of her, they wandered left and right, peering momentarily from one dark shadow to another. When she was younger, these woods had been a welcomed refuge for imaginary adventures. And maybe in broad daylight, she would have felt the same way about them. Now, however, they were menacing and suffocating.

This discrepancy between how Stephanie felt about days and nights was something that had been growing for months. She felt a split within herself. During the comforting light of days, she was generally happy and content. But when the sun set, she could not escape the sense of fear that crept over her. It made her feel childish. Over the months, it had worn her down to the point that even during the day while she felt safe she could not keep from thinking about each coming night. She'd grown more withdrawn and depressed. She eventually realized that the most distressing thing was not being able to talk to anyone about all of this. She knew the stories in town. It was hard to escape speculations about where that man had gone, or who had taken that boy, Tommy. So she kept her fears to herself. But even as she had finished up her second semester at Wellesley College, she found that she hated crossing campus at night. She found herself studying late in the library; sometimes, she even wandered its open interior architecture and suspended walkways that crisscrossed the building to kill time, waiting until someone she knew seemed headed out towards the dorms. Some nights she was lucky, other nights she wasn't.

A subtle rustle from somewhere in the trees off to her right caught her attention. She picked up her pace. An icy chill spread through her chest as she heard the rustling matching pace with her. In an instant of brash bravado, Stephanie stopped. The rustling stopped too. There's someone there!

Willing herself forward, Stephanie continued to walk quickly. She reached the yard and headed straight for the front steps. Stopping, she turned back to look at the woods. One part of her brain could hear what her father would say: it's probably a deer—though it might be a coyote. But the other part of her brain, the primal part responsible for the drive to survive, felt sure that lurking in the deep shadows of those woods was something much more sinister than a coyote. She stared into the blackness and felt sure she could feel something staring back at her.

Unable to will her body to stay there another moment, she turned and bolted up the steps. Reaching the front door, she ripped open the screen door and produced her keys. She unlocked the door and flung herself inside the house before she could give much thought to the hour. It was nearly ten thirty. Her parents, both prone to rising early, were no doubt asleep. She wondered if she'd been too loud. Pausing, she listened to the quiet house. She could hear the faint sounds of the old TV on in her parents' room. Only the light over the kitchen sink glowed downstairs. This was what her mother always did when she was out. She crossed to the kitchen and extinguished the light. The darkness felt immediately oppressive. She turned it back on and opted to pull out her cell phone to use as a makeshift flashlight.

She crept up the wooden stairs, trying to keep them from creaking too loudly, though no amount of effort prevented them from creaking to some degree. In the stillness of the house, each creak and pop seemed amplified. Reaching the top of the stairs, she immediately headed for her parents' room. As she expected, she found them both in bed, fast asleep, the TV still playing an old movie on cable. She quietly reached over to the television and turned it off. Her mother stirred slightly, but made no other sound. Stephanie hesitated for a moment, looking at her sleeping mother. An urge to wake her swept over her. But why? What did she need exactly? What would she say to her? She was nineteen, not nine. Somehow, claiming to be scared of ... of what? What did she think was outside? Now that she was inside, she wondered if her mind had just been playing tricks on her. You're just being silly, she told herself. And with that, she turned and left the room.

SHE SPAT THE FOAMING toothpaste out and rinsed her mouth. Standing in the bathroom now in shorts and a tank top, she looked in the mirror. She reached back and brushed aside her dark hair. Her fingers hovered above the scar on her neck. She touched it. A pulse like a low-level electric shock shot through her neck and back. She removed her hand and just stared into the mirror. Somewhere in the house, something creaked. Her eyes shot to the door she'd left ajar. You're letting your mind run wild now, she told herself. The sooner you just go to bed, the sooner you can just be done with this night. But was that all she could hope for from now on? To get through nights so that she could lead a perfectly happy and seemingly normal life during the day? Standing in the bathroom in the middle of the night feeling creeped out, either by her own active imagination or by something else, she realized that this was not the time or place to work that out. She forced herself to leave the bathroom. She exited and shut off the light. Though the distance to her room was short, she felt every inch of that darkness as though she'd been plunged into murky dark waters with no sense of how deep it reached.

In her room, she quickly turned on her bedside lamp. She climbed in bed and looked over at the window. A light breeze caused the curtains to wave slightly. She cursed her father for being too cheap to install air conditioning. It was too warm tonight to dare to close the window. But it was clearly one of those nights for Stephanie: a bad night. Every now and then, she had these. Her methods of muddling her way through the night varied. She glanced over at the lamp by her bed and the alarm clock that sat below it. It was now nearly eleven. There was still a lot of night ahead of her. Leaving the lamp on, Stephanie rolled over and forced herself to close her eyes. Just go to sleep. Everything will feel different tomorrow. It always does.

SHE HAD NO RECOLLECTION of when exactly she might have drifted off to sleep, but she must have been asleep. Now she was awake, suddenly.

She looked around without stirring from her place in bed. She was still on her side. Her lamp was still on. But she faced away from the lamp and clock. So she had no way of knowing what time it was or how long she might have been out. But the air felt cooler. She must have been asleep for a while at least.

A faint tapping sound somewhere behind her caused her muscles to tighten and goose bumps to travel up her arms. There was that feeling again, that feeling of being watched. She turned herself over quickly, unsure of what she would see, but hoping to see nothing at all. Her room as it normally looked confronted her. Her stuffed animals were on the old dresser, her closet door securely closed, her mirror in the corner ... she hated the mirror. Something about mirrors at night ...

She took a deep breath and tried to relax. Laying back down in bed, she looked over at her alarm clock. It was now 2:58 AM. She had definitely been asleep, and for a while too. That was the good news. The bad news was that being only about three AM, there was a lot of night ahead of her still. And of course, this part of such nights was always the longest. Sometimes she would just lay awake unsure of what had unsettled her. Had she dreamed? Other times, she knew she'd heard things, felt things, seen things. She pushed all such thoughts from her head. Now was not the time to think about anything like that. She had to get her mind on something else, anything else. An old urge she hadn't felt in years crept up. Should she say a prayer? Her parents, still being "church folk," as she had once described them to her college roommate, had brought her up with some semblance of religious tradition. But she had let all of that drift away from her—or she away from it—some time ago. It wasn't the first time the thought occurred to her on a night like this. But she never knew what to say. Instead she just stared at her clock. The minute digit changed from eight to nine.

Her lamp flickered! Faint tapping sounds emitted from the far corner of her room. Stephanie felt the cold flow of fear race through her body. They're here! She laid on her back, trying to control her breathing. She gripped the sheets of her bed. More tapping. Her lamp flickered again. Then, it went out!

Darkness swallowed her. It couldn't have been more than a split second, but in that time, Stephanie wondered if she should run. But as the thought occurred to her, a bright blue light suddenly shone through her window. The light travelled up the floor, over the bed, and across her body. A pressure crept over Stephanie's entire body as she lay there. She couldn't move!

She was lifted from her bed, head and shoulders first, her feet remaining on the bed for the moment. Her fingers were forced to open and release the sheets. Her arms remained stiff, still outstretched where her hands had been gripping her sheets. She was standing, arms out, facing the window now. Only, there was no weight on her feet. She floated forward, off the bed, and towards the window. Her heart raced; she desperately wanted to scream, to make this stop. Only her frantic eyes could move, searching left and right for any means to stop her slow approach to the window.

An oppressive hum droned now. The light grew brighter and the hum louder. It hurt her eyes, but she couldn't close them. Tears streamed down her cheeks, yet brighter still the light grew as she was pulled closer to it by some unknown force, some invisible hand that both pulled her from her bed and slowly squeezed her body tighter in the process. She couldn't breathe. The light grew brighter still, until there was nothing but the blinding light and the deafening hum.

KAREN KNEW BETTER, BUT she was so annoyed with her husband that she couldn't help herself. She looked down at her cell phone screen even as she drove down the rural New Hampshire road, the familiar sight of trees and the White Mountains in the distance at the moment forgotten. Instead, she read the last text from her husband: "No time, had to give them money for lunch."

She swore under her breath and glanced up at the road. Then she looked back down and began to type out her furious message. She doubted that her son would end up being able to have lunch at all with his gluten allergy. What would be available to buy at the day camp? Would they have accounted for food allergies? How many times had she told her husband to pack her son and daughter a lunch? She managed to tap out the words, "What will Devon eat?" and then she glanced up at the road.

She screamed and slammed on her breaks, jerking the steering wheel hard to the right. A person stood in the middle of the road! The tires screeched and her Jeep Grand Cherokee leaned forward and a little to the left with the force of fighting so much inertia. Her seatbelt held her in place. The SUV rocked back as it reached its sudden stop.

Karen looked out her window. She hadn't hit the person. They still stood a few yards back in the middle of the road. It was a girl, by the looks of it, maybe a teenager. Her dark hair blew in the breeze. Karen threw on her hazard lights and got out of her car, her sudden panic instantly exploding into rage.

"What the hell do you think you're doing?" she screamed at the girl. "I could have killed you!"

She marched up to the girl, but as she approached, she noticed that the girl wore only a tank top and shorts. Her feet were bare. Judging from how dirty they were, she'd been walking for a while. What's more, it seemed the shorts and tank were inside-out. The tag on the back of her shorts fluttered in the light breeze as Karen approached her. The girl still faced away. She took a shaky step forward on her stained bare feet.

"Hey, are you okay?" Karen said, her tone now suddenly changed again, given her new shock and concern. She walked around the girl and found that she stared off into the distance, her eyes icy and vacant. "Are you on drugs?" she asked. But Karen got no response from the girl, so she reached out and touched her arm.

The girl's eyes snapped to Karen's hand and then up to her eyes with sharp focus. She opened her mouth and let out a deafening scream! Karen stumbled back, falling on the road. Pain shot through her elbow where it landed hard on the asphalt. The girl continued to scream with such primal ferocity that Karen forgot everything else. She scrambled away from the girl and back to her Jeep. Reaching inside, she found her cell phone. The girl's scream ceased, but the echo of it bounced out through the woods and haunted Karen's ears. It was as if the scream had silenced the surrounding world. Even the breeze seemed to die off. On her cell, she punched in three numbers she had not dialed in a long time: 911.

CHAPTER TWO

NICOLE MITCHELL PUSHED THROUGH the aches. Her feet struck the sidewalk, setting the rhythm to her run. To her right, the Charles River separated Boston from Cambridge. She glanced at the Boston skyline from her vantage point in Cambridge. The muscles in her legs burned. Thin lines of sweat traveled down her face. How long had she been running? It had to have been at least forty minutes if she was now by the river.

She slowed her pace to a walk as she breathed hard. She pulled out her headphones, the music suddenly vanishing and the sounds of the city flooded her. Other Sunday morning joggers ran past her. She pulled out her cell phone and stopped the music. Chopin ... probably not what other joggers were listening to, she figured. But Mitchell found that vanishing into various flavors of classical music allowed her mind to focus on other things while she ran. She often worked through details of a case this way.

Replacing her phone into the armband of her running shirt, she turned and started walking back the way she had come. Normally, she would not have run out this far. But these days, why not? She had nowhere to be just now, and being back in her apartment didn't sound very appealing on a warm summer day. Maybe she would go back and shower and then go out again. But go do what? The real nagging question she desperately tried to keep her mind from fixating on was: When can I start working again?

Eventually, the slow pace of walking bothered her and she was back to running. Her headphones back in, she was now on Mozart. Within the hour, she was back to Somerville. Turning on to her street, she slowed again to a walk and pulled out her headphones again. Her lungs ached with the long and vigorous run, but she ignored them. As she approached her apartment, she spotted someone sitting on the front steps of the old three story red brick building. The man, dressed in a suit, dark skin and even darker curly hair, looked up from his phone.

"There you are," Agent Brown smiled at her and stood.

"What are you doing here, Anthony?" She said, trying to keep her tone as matter of fact as possible, but wondered if subtle hints of excitement had shown through anyway.

"Thought I'd pay you a visit and see if you might make me one of those terrible milkshakes of yours," Brown said with a mischievous glint in his eyes.

"I told you it was a protein shake," she said, approaching. "But that's what you get for taking what's not yours."

"Hey, whatever. It was there and it was ..." he looked up in a mock gesture of deep thought as if searching for the right word. "... just awful! Seriously, what was in that?"

Mitchell shook her head, letting out a slight laugh. "How about water?"

THE DOOR TO MITCHELL'S APARTMENT swung open and she and Brown walked in. Brown closed the door behind him. The apartment was small with hardwood floors. An island separated the kitchen from the small space designated as the dining room. A small table with four chairs sat there under a tiny gold chandelier. Mitchell pulled out one of the chairs and took a seat so she could remove her running shoes.

"Damn, girl," Brown remarked, looking around. "I don't think I've ever seen the place this clean before."

Mitchell stood and set her shoes by the door. "Nothing better to do."

"What if you had something better?" Brown asked.

Mitchell turned to him, trying to read his expression. He tried to maintain a blank face, but there was no point. Good, she thought. I can finally get back to work!

"Am I back on duty?" she played along.

Brown bobbed his head the way she'd seen him do before when he meant to say more or less. "Eh, sort of." He said. "Remember that case last year with the missing kid up in New Hampshire?"

Stupid question. Mitchell grinned. "Like I'd forget."

"Well, there might be something new for you to look into."

This got Mitchell's attention. What was going on? Her mind immediately jumped to the worst case scenario. "Another kid missing?"

"Well, not missing," Brown shrugged. "Anymore. And not exactly a kid. College girl was snatched from her bedroom last night. Turned up about eleven miles from home hours later. She was totally disoriented."

"Clothing on inside out?" Mitchell ventured.

Brown nodded, "Yep."

"Did she remember anything?"

"Not a thing. Just a bright light," he offered. He paused before saying the next words: "But it's North Woodstock again."

Sonofabitch! So it's happening again. Mitchell looked off, lost in thought, too many questions racing through her head. Brown watched her, waiting. Finally, he spoke again.

"Little grey men from outer space?"

Brought back to the moment, Mitchell shook her head. "No such thing. But sounds an awful lot like the Tommy Ferguson case last year." She locked on to Brown's eyes, trying to work out what he was getting at. "So, the Bureau is sending us up?"

Brown smiled now. "As much as I would love nothing more than driving all over New Hampshire chasing UFOs with you, we can't spare anyone. Lot of pressure on the FBI since Jeff's ..." His smile vanished. Suddenly, he couldn't hold her gaze anymore. His eyes wandered down to the floor. "Shit! You know ... I'm sorry. I should have asked you first how you're even doing."

Mitchell shrugged. He looked at her again, but his whole demeanor changed now. She could almost see him walking on the shards of eggshells scattered through his mind.

"Nicole, you know no one blames you," he began. "So you shouldn't blame yourself either."

But the way he looked off made Mitchell wonder what he knew that he wasn't telling her. She didn't want to push it right now, however. Best stick to the something she could actually deal with. And by the sound of it, something she was actually being asked to deal with.

"So what?" she carried on. "I'm going alone?"

"Just to check in on things," Brown confirmed. "See if this has any possible connection to the missing boy last year. You feel up to it?"

Mitchell allowed herself a slight smile at the question. Feel up to it? She'd been itching to get back to work for a while now. Hell, she would have welcomed being called back into headquarters to sit at a desk and do paperwork at this point. But this ... the potential for an actual investigation, and this of all cases too. She was going to do things differently this time. She needed a new approach, a different method of attack. She could sense Brown watching her, waiting for an answer.

"Yeah," she said. "I just ..."

"What's up?"

She knew this was likely asking a lot—maybe even too much. "Can I hire an outside consultant?"

Brown's lips parted, his right eyebrow coming down first in his usual mode of amusement. "What kind of consultant?"

"Just trust me."

Brown pressed his lips together, thinking. But Mitchell already knew her plan of attack. She'd get her way. She was sure of it.

DIEGO SILVA PULLED UP to the Clark residence in his pick-up. A North Woodstock Police cruiser was parked next to the sedan that belonged to Tim and Dorothy. Diego was careful to park his truck on the other side of the two cars so that the cruiser could leave at any time. Getting out of his truck, he checked his dress pants and dress shirt in case any dirt from his truck had gotten on him. As he did so, he heard the screen door slap shut on the house. Looking up, he found Officer Silvia O'Conner walking down the steps towards him. She was one of the newer officers on the North Woodstock police force, but Diego made a point of getting around town and getting to know as many people as possible. O'Conner had always struck him as kind and sincere. She was in her early thirties, relatively fit, and had an easy going way about her. But

Diego had also seen her arrest a few unruly characters before, and knew that she knew how, when, and where to take off the gloves.

"Good morning, Pastor Diego," she said with her usual warmth. "Sunday service over already?"

Diego approached her. He spoke in his accent that, along with his golden brown skin, revealed his Brazilian origin. "No no. Just wrapping up. I excused myself early so I could come be with the Clarks. How are they?"

"Positively freaked out," O'Conner remarked. "What is this, third time this has happened?"

"Fourth," Diego offered. "But it's been a while."

The front door of the Clark's house swung open again and out came Chief of Police Harvey Wilson. Wilson had his own charm, but seemed a little gruffer with age. Now into his late fifties, his beard was more salt than pepper. His deep-set eyes looked out at the world more often than not with a twinge of hesitation. But most folks in town had nothing but good things to say about him—except those who Wilson had caught breaking laws who still refused to believe they'd done anything wrong.

"O'Conner, what do you say we go visit Stephanie's friends," He called out as he walked down the steps before noticing Diego standing there. "Well, good morning, Pastor. Dorothy will be happy to see you." He walked over to them.

"Why do you need to speak to Stephanie's friends?" Diego probed.

"Just want to chat a little," Wilson shrugged. "Stephanie was with some friends last night, but the girls dropped her off here before going to a movie."

"Stephanie insists they had nothing to do with any of this," O'Conner volunteered. "They dropped her off hours before this happened."

Chief Wilson shot her a look. Diego figured while Wilson liked to keep as warm of a demeanor as possible, he hated offering up too much information. Diego recalled the first time he had met Wilson a few years ago. "The good thing about small towns," Wilson had said to him, "is that everyone knows each other. It's also the bad thing. News travels fast. Good or bad. True ... or false."

Wilson just scratched his beard and mumbled, "Yep, but gotta' talk to everyone. Just good police work. If you'll excuse us, Pastor, we best be going."

He headed for the police cruiser. O'Conner smiled and said goodbye and followed. Diego watched them go. Then turning to the house, he walked up the steps. As he did so, it seemed to him that a dark cloud passed by the sun. He thought the forecast had called for clear skies today. Looking around, he could see the sun shining still. But all the same, it was as if the world felt a little darker all of a sudden.

"Pastor Diego?" came Dorothy's voice.

He turned and found the middle-aged woman standing at her door, both surprise and fatigue evident on her face. She wore no make-up nor a dress as Diego might have seen on any other Sunday morning. Instead, her face seemed pale and gaunt. She wore shorts and a faded shirt she probably only wore at home or in the garden.

Dorothy swung the door open and insisted he come in. Diego complied. She announced to her husband that their pastor was here and then excused herself to fetch Stephanie from her room. Tim came in from the living room and shook Diego's hand, distractedly thanking him for coming out. Tim worked at the bank in Lincoln. He was a tall, balding man with a firm handshake and confident smile. But this morning, he seemed weak and distant, lost in some internal fog. Dorothy returned with Stephanie and they all moved to the living room where Dorothy, a retired teacher who seemed to constantly be watching out for other people's needs, proceeded through her normal mode of hospitality. She insisted on asking Diego if he needed tea, or anything to eat, or water, or maybe a soda? Politely, Diego insisted she sit down. He was here to care for them, not the other way around.

"Of course, of course," Dorothy said, seeming embarrassed.

The Clarks took the sofa. Stephanie sat nestled between her father and mother. Pastor Diego sat across from them in the creaky old recliner. He sat poised on its edge, leaning in to hear Stephanie, who spoke softly. Dorothy had her hand on Stephanie's back, rubbing it gently and watching her with attentive eyes. Tim, her father, stared down at his own hands, which were folded together before him. He too sat forward, elbows on the knees of his faded jeans, his bald spot all that faced Diego.

At first, Diego asked only simple questions about how Stephanie felt. He asked about what she'd been doing last night. Stephanie's answers were short and nondescript. She'd been out with friends. They had grabbed ice cream, then they decided to go to a movie. Stephanie didn't want to go. Finally, he asked her about what had happened to her last night. Stephanie looked to her mother, then down to the floor.

"I don't really know for sure," she said.

"Do you remember anything that happened?" Diego pushed lightly.

"We've been over this with Chief Wilson already," Tim said, maintaining politeness, though not enough to hide his true feelings about Diego's questions.

Diego had to remind himself that not everyone wanted the type of hands-on personal care from their pastor he loved so much. And certainly the Clarks had just been through an awful lot.

"I understand," he said. "I really just want to be of help in any way I can."

"I just remember the light," Stephanie spoke up suddenly, still staring down at the floor. "I couldn't move. It picked me up right out of my bed. The light kept getting brighter. And then ... there was nothing. I woke up on the road. That woman was there on her phone calling 911."

Tim looked up to Diego. "She really should rest. We appreciate you coming out, but I think she should sleep now."

"Of course," Diego relented. "Maybe we could pray for her first?

Dorothy glanced at her husband with expectant eyes. It was Tim's turn to relent. He nodded.

CHAPTER THREE

Sᴏ̨ᴜɪɴᴛɪɴɢ ɪɴ ᴛʜᴇ ʙʟɪɴᴅɪɴɢ light, he wondered just why the hell he had bothered with this? Right about now he could have been sitting in his condo in Cambridge sipping coffee and reading while the Red Sox game was on in the background. Instead, here he was. But he knew the answer: His book wasn't about to promote itself. He clicked the tiny remote that advanced his Keynote presentation to the next slide. He moved to the side so he wasn't looking so directly into the projector's beam and immediately regretted this. It didn't matter how many times he looked out at the chairs set up in this local bookstore, the sting of disappointment didn't lessen. The chairs among the bookshelves could easily have sat forty or more people. Currently only nine people sat scattered about. At least half of them were buried in their smart phones or tablets. One or one hundred, he told himself. Just do your thing and go home.

"This subject," Dr. Alan Evans continued his presentation, gesturing to the picture of a severely bruised woman in a hospital gown now on the screen. "Had long periods in a catatonic state, had seizures, and inflicted injuries on herself."

With the room so empty and quiet, he couldn't help but notice a newcomer in the back approach and stop, standing at a distance. But he reminded himself to remain focused on his material. If nothing else, this would serve as more practice until he could land a conference. That is, if book sales picked up.

"Medication and therapy over four months reversed her condition." He clicked the remote again and a new picture of the same woman appeared. But now she was smiling, unbruised, and wearing dress pants and a cardigan. "This is the patient today. We were able to determine that both chemical imbalances in her brain and repressed childhood abuses had contributed to her illness. In spite of claims that her house was haunted, since her treatment there have been no recurrences of the events that led to her condition."

A hand in the audience shot up. A little taken a back, Evans squinted out at the man whose hand had broken his train of thought. "Yes?"

"You suggest in your book that the first step to helping such patients is to approach such problems on their own terms," the male audience member said. "Isn't this essentially pandering to their delusions that such paranormal hocus-pocus is real?"

Evans smiled. This question. Always this fucking question.

"First of all, thanks for reading my book. If you'll recall, I explained in my book that there is no use in initiating therapy from an attacking position if the patient sincerely believes what they are experiencing is paranormal. But the objective is to move them towards the recognition that such things are products of the subconscious mind in its effort to cope with painful memories or manifestations of complicated medical conditions."

Evans could read the unconvinced face of the man. But before he could continue, a second hand shot up on the other side of the room. Well, I guess it's Q&A time already, he thought. Fine, let's just get on with it then.

"Uh, yes?" Evans turned to the new questioner.

This time it was a middle-aged woman. "But, Dr. Evans," she began, unable or uninterested in hiding her combative tone. "Is there any room in your thinking for the remote possibility that some paranormal events may in fact be legitimate? Or is every supernatural or spiritual occurrence to be explained away as just happening in the patient's head?"

The man who'd asked the first question emitted a groan. It was a loaded question. No doubt she'd been waiting for an opportunity to ask it. He wondered if she'd heard anything he had presented so far. He doubted that she'd ever read his book. She probably had just read a few witty customer reviews on Amazon and felt informed enough to relegate him to a particular category in her mind. Well, okay, thought Evans. He had not expected this question, but this might be good. This just might allow him to reinforce his commitment to empirical science that seemed so increasingly hard for many readers and critics of his book to grasp. Even some fellow psychiatrists and psychologists had begun to question his methods as he didn't immediately throw out the profound shaping power of the subjective experience of his patients when it came to the "paranormal." One day he'd write a book about American pop culture's unhealthy fixation with insisting everything be seen as a system of hard facts with no mystery. But of course, even he thought most "paranormal" experiences were ludicrous. It wasn't that science couldn't explain such things. It was simply a matter that current science might not always be fully equipped to understand such things in the moment. After all, the pop-empirical crowd who loved to spout off facts in arguments about nutrition, vaccination, and even evolution seemed to constantly forget that the history of science is one of constant revisions and refinements as new evidence overturns old ideas.

"My work in neuroscience and therapy are based on evidence and empirical data," he said calmly. "I don't think we help our patients by entertaining ideas of ghosts, or demons, or past lives, or little grey men from outer space."

"Then why not immediately address this with the patient?" the first questioner piped up again.

Shit. Back to this question. Evans forced a grin and moved out from behind the podium so he could get further away from the projector's beam. Why was it so hard to exist in the middle? His mind raced as he sought out the most casual and composed manner for responding to this question in a way that might satisfy both concerns.

"This is where I believe I need to be sensitive to my patients' needs. While ultimately I believe there is a logical and scientific explanation for every paranormal event a patient claims to have experienced, to them in the moment of experiencing such things, the paranormal is very real, and they are experiencing these things for a reason. I just want to get to that reason without forcing my own ideas upon them.

"You see, we are the product of our perceptions. For better or worse, how we see the world fundamentally shapes us. So if my patient truly believes they are the reincarnation of Jack the Ripper, there is a sense in which to them in that moment, it is true. So first I need to peel back the layers of what brings about this false perception. Then, and only then, can I help them deal with the source of this false perception."

"Or simply introduce them to a new false perception," the second questioner jumped in now.

Evans sighed. He knew her type. She was a pseudo-scientific new ager who spewed feel good bullshit to any moron willing to listen while she jumped from one new idea to the next. Down the road her type inevitably found that their lives were still hopelessly depressing compared to the unrealistically rosy picture they had in their minds of what their affluent first world lives informed by hipster materialism, horoscopes, meditation, and hippy therapists should be. An interesting breed for sure, but Evans wasn't about to try to deconstruct that right now for these nine people.

"My goal is to help people," he stood his ground, half hoping the woman caught the implications of what that statement inferred about her goals. "I don't see how entertaining superstitions and delusions of grandeur brings healing to anyone."

He could see the anger in the woman's eyes. He glanced down at his watch and checked the time. "Well, I've already gone over my time," he lied—but it wasn't like he was about to sell any books today anyway. "Thank you all for being here this morning."

Without any protest or complaint, everyone got up.

SHE'D SNUCK INTO THE bookstore and waited while Dr. Evans completed his talk. Nicole, now in a sleek black suit, her long light hair flowing past her shoulders, felt relieved to be back in the familiarity of her life as an agent. She wondered how much Anthony had picked up on her state of sheer boredom. There was only so much TV she could watch, only so long she could read a novel before becoming restless and actually missing reading case files, and there were only so many runs she could go on. It wasn't that she longed for the tedious aspects of bureaucratic law enforcement. It was the frustrating sense of being stuck, unproductive. She could have visited her mother more. But she couldn't stand the constant kind eyes of her mother watching her every move, wondering how she was, always seeking to talk over things again and again when all that Nicole really wanted was for life to get back to normal.

This felt more like it! A reason to put on a bit of makeup, a suit she hadn't worn in a month, and having something to investigate. She was, however, surprised to see Dr. Evans's book signing so sparsely attended. She listened to the exchange between a couple of the audience members and Evans, smiling at Evans's poise while being hassled from two sides. This was exactly why she was here.

Evans concluded the presentation. Mitchell watched as the nine scattered people got up. Some stretched, others headed off to peruse the shelves. She overhead one man say to another he was walking out with, "We should have just gone to brunch like usual." The man he was with just laughed in reply.

Evans gathered his things from the podium and headed back to a table set up at the back of the room where several copies of his book sat out. Setting his messenger bag down, Evans began to pack up his books into a larger duffle bag that waited under the table. Mitchell approached him.

"Aren't you packing up too soon? Might want to sell a few copies to your adoring fans," she said as she stopped before the table.

Evans looked up, amused. His expression changed to surprise. Then a genuine smile. "Agent Mitchell. I didn't expect to see you here."

"Can I buy you a cup of coffee?" Mitchell asked. "Or maybe a couple of shots, after that reception."

Evans laughed, then shook his head, "As appealing as either coffee or hard liquor sound right now—and they do—I really can't. Not kosher for me to fraternize with former patients. Especially one I only just cleared for duty."

"And if I told you it was official FBI business?" Mitchell countered.

Evans grew serious, considering her words. Light jazz music

sprinkled out of the overhead speakers in the bookstore. The room was empty now, except for them.

THE SMELL OF ESPRESSO and freshly brewed coffee filled the small place. A grinder kicked on, reducing more espresso beans to a fine powder. Evans stared out the coffee shop's large windows from where he sat at a small table. People walked by, soaking in the warm summer day in Boston. The tourists with guidebooks and recently purchased Boston paraphernalia moved at their slow pace—presumably following the Freedom Trail—while the locals maintained a faster speed, Sunday or not. Alan thought about being back at his condo with the paper out and the game on. Guess that's not happening now.

Agent Mitchell approached, bearing two cups of coffee. She set one before Alan and took a seat across from him.

"Thanks for the coffee," Evans said. "So how have you been since our last appointment?"

Mitchell looked out the window as well. "Fine," she said. But Evans read in her tone a desire to avoid such a conversation.

"Sleeping better?" He pushed just a little.

Mitchell looked back and forced a crooked smile. "Getting there."

Okay, he was done pushing. And he wasn't on the clock anyway. He sensed Mitchell's longing to dive into whatever she really was there to talk about. But he suspected she was also too polite to barge into the matter so quickly. And of course, he was curious himself.

"So, official FBI business, huh?" he opened the door for her.

She leaned forward slightly, squaring her shoulders up to him. "Yeah. I need your help with a case. And I think it's something you might be uniquely able to help me with."

"Okay. I'm listening."

"I've got a girl—a young woman, really—in New Hampshire who claims she was abducted by aliens last night."

Evans nodded slowly. Well, she's done her homework on me. "She believes what exactly?"

"She went missing from her home last night around 3:00 AM. This morning, a woman driving down a country road eleven miles from the girl's house nearly hit her. The girl was just walking down the middle of the road. According to the case file I was given, she claims to have been abducted in the past as well. She also claims to have an implant in her neck."

Evans took all of this in. It sounded similar to cases he had studied and a couple he had personally encountered in his work as a therapist. Agent Mitchell reached down to her bag and produced a file folder. Laying it down on the table, she opened it and flipped through its papers until she found a picture of a young woman with dark hair and a pale complexion.

"This is Stephanie Clark," she said, turning the photo so he could see her better. "She just finished her freshman year at Wellesley College. She's only nineteen. She lives with her mother and father in North Woodstock, New Hampshire. That's close to Lincoln, or an hour north of Concord. Her mother is a retired elementary school teacher. Her father works at the bank in Lincoln. They have been a part of the community for almost their whole lives. This is the first time the police have been called because of her … experiences."

"She never called the police before this?" Evans looked up from the photo.

"She was never returned anywhere other than home. And never gone for more than a few hours during the night. In those other cases, her parents didn't even know she was gone until she said something to them the next day. But in this case, the woman who found her called 911. And her parents woke up to find she was not in her bed."

Mitchell grabbed another photo and slid it over to him. This one was of the back of Stephanie's neck where a slight lump could be seen just to the right of the spine. "Local police took this photo this morning. She claims she's had it for a few months."

"What does she say it is?" Evans asked.

"Something they put in her. But otherwise she doesn't know," Mitchell shrugged and took the photos back. "All she's said is it hurts sometimes. And when it hurts, it's usually because they're close."

Evans sipped his coffee thinking. Then he asked, "Any evidence of childhood trauma?"

"That's what I need your help finding out," Mitchell smiled. "There are other cases in the area. A year ago, a young boy went missing. He had been abducted several times. He had similar markings on his body. He was always taken at night. And initially he was always returned to his home. But then he started being dropped off further and further from home. The abductions became more frequent. Then one night, he was just gone."

"He claimed aliens were abducting him too?"

Mitchell nodded. "According to a therapist who performed hypnosis on him, he had repressed memories of his abduction experiences. It fits the scenario established by other cases."

"Yeah," Evans stared down at his coffee, thinking. Then he looked up suddenly as a new question occurred to him, "You believe this?"

Mitchell shook her head. "Like you, I think there's a logical explanation for all of this. But I've done my homework. And, as far as alien abduction cases go ... this fits all the criteria. On top of that, over the past five years, there have been eight people between the ages of nine and nineteen that have gone missing in the area. There was also a local drunk that went missing, but it's hard to know if there was any legitimacy to his claims of being abducted. All the same, there have been numerous people who claim to have seen UFOs or alien beings. Something's going on up there."

She looked down at the files, then her coffee. Evans waited, watching her. She seemed lost in thought for a moment. Finally, she looked up, leaning in closer. She spoke more softly now.

"Is it possible that a person or a group of people could be using the suggestion of UFOs as a means to kidnap these kids?"

Evans raised his eyebrows, considering this. "Now that's a big claim. Got anything that might substantiate that?"

"Right now, it's just a theory. I need your help getting to the bottom of this. Stephanie's case fits the M.O. of abductions. I want to know if someone could be behind this," she paused, looking at him. "And if so, I want to stop them."

Evans noticed the creased lines that seemed to appear out of thin air around Mitchell's eyes. Were they always there? Or did they just appear now that she frowned slightly with the gravity of the case at hand. She must understand the boldness, the complexities, of her theory, he thought. But she's committed. Evans sat back in his chair, letting out a sigh. He looked off and considered his options. Did he have time for this? Did he dare get mixed up in this? It wasn't technically kosher for him to be working so closely with a patient he'd just been seeing, even if their work was officially concluded. But another thought nagged at him. Was this exactly the potential credibility he needed? The FBI calling upon him.

"Nicole," he said softly, "It's not ..."

"I know what you're thinking," she said. "This really mucks up our patient-therapist relationship. But we're both professionals here. I wouldn't be asking you if I didn't honestly believe you could help me break this case wide open. There's something going on here, and we can help this girl. We need to help this girl."

Evans nodded, then sighed. "I'll need to check my schedule," he said. "Maybe I could come up next week."

Mitchell shook her head again, "It'll be too late. We need to talk to this girl before anything else happens."

"You think she might vanish too?" Evans filled in the gaps. "Like the boy?"

"It's happened before," she said. "Look, I know I'm asking a lot. But I need your help to stop this."

Evans pressed his lips together, still tasting the bitterness of his coffee on his tongue. "When do we leave?"

"How quickly can you pack?" Mitchell asked, without missing a beat.

CHAPTER FOUR

WATER RAINED DOWN ON her. It was quite hot, though never hot enough. Stephanie stood under the cascade of the shower. Her right hand pressed against the tile wall as she steadied herself. The cold of the tile seemed to reach into her skin and crawl up her arm. For a brief moment, her heart raced, feeling some unknown and yet familiar panic. She withdrew her hand and wrapped her arms around her chest. She was alone at home, safely locked in the bathroom in the shower she'd used for years. But suddenly, she felt the uncontrollable desire to cover herself, as if even here, she was being watched.

She reached a hand back and touched the bump on her neck. It was tender and sore. Staring down at the water that made its way down the drain, she wondered when she would have the will power to do anything other than stand there. She wasn't even sure how long she had been standing there already, simply letting the shower run hot water over her. It was getting harder these days to keep track of time. At last, she managed to force herself to move. With effort, she carried out the required tasks to accomplish a proper shower. But it was as if invisible weights were tied to her arms. Every movement felt difficult and slow.

Turning the flow of water off, she stepped out of the shower and wrapped a towel around herself. Heading to her room, she tried to find something to wear. But making decisions seemed so difficult as well. Finally giving up, she settled on a rather uninspired and ratty tank-top and jean shorts. It wasn't like she was about to set foot out of the house. Comfort in the summer heat seemed to her the only relevant criteria at the moment.

She pulled the shorts on. As she ran her fingers around the waistband, she felt a sudden sharp sting on her back. Moving to the mirror in the corner, she twisted her body so she could try to see what was causing the pain. She pulled back the waistband for her shorts and panties. Right at the waistline were three red marks in a triangle. These marks were new! She touched the marks and felt the surge of pain.

Drawing closer to the mirror, she tried to twist for a better view. Not quite able to get a better look, she tried to adjust the mirror. As she did so, for a split second her eyes caught something in the room behind her. It was one of them! She screamed, spinning about to face the intruder. She stumbled back, running into the mirror and knocking it against the wall. She caught herself in time to keep from falling into the mirror and causing serious harm. But her eyes searched the room.

The empty room.

But she'd seen him—it—whatever they were. She'd clearly seen the slender shape of grey shoulders, the thin neck, leading up to that oblong head. But it was those eyes—completely black eyes—that truly made her skin crawl. They were like shark eyes, only much larger.

She frantically looked about the room, not daring to move. On the dresser sat her collection of teddy bears. Her room was as she always recalled it. It couldn't have been her imagination, could it? The door to her room opened, causing her to jump again. She screamed again. Her mother rushed into the room, her eyes wide, her face white.

"What is it?" Dorothy asked.

Stephanie looked at her mother, dumfounded. Slowly, relief washed over her. She stood up straight, trying to control her breathing. Her heart pounded inside her rib cage. With every beat, her hands shook and pain shot through her head. A distant ringing in her ears took over.

"Stephanie? Are you okay?" her mother approached her. "Sweetie, what is it?"

Stephanie fought to formulate words. Finally, she whispered, "I ... saw something."

She only noticed she was crying when the tears slipping down her face tickled her neck.

NORTHBOUND ON 93, MITCHELL sat behind the wheel of her black Accord. Dr. Evans sat in the passenger seat, his cell phone pressed to his ear as he looked out the window. "No. I understand, Cindy," he said into his phone. "It's just that the FBI has requested my help on an active investigation that's time sensitive." He paused, listening. "I know. Just please, call my appointments and clear my schedule for the next two days." Another pause. "Thank you, Cindy. I'll call if anything changes. Yeah, that's fine. Okay. Bye." He hung up and looked over at Mitchell.

"She's a good receptionist," he explained. "Just hates surprises."

Mitchell smiled. "Sorry to put you through this."

"It's fine," Evans waived off the apology. "I was thinking I should get out of town for a while anyway after that so-called book signing. How long were you there?"

"Caught just the end," Mitchell said.

"Oh, so definitely the best part," Evans chuckled.

"Not everyone there seemed too thrilled with your work."

"Haven't found my fan base yet, you might say," Evans shrugged with a wry smile. "Anything that bumps up against the label of 'paranormal' tends to elicit strong feelings one way or another. From the few that bother to actually engage. Most are more comfortable ignoring such things."

"So I guess the book isn't flying off the shelves, huh?" Mitchell ventured a friendly jab.

Evans smiled and shook his head. "Nope. Maybe it will once I go to the UFO convention in Roswell."

Mitchell glanced over at him. Was he serious? He'd said it seriously enough. "Really?"

"Kidding," he grinned. "I'm especially unpopular with UFO enthusiasts."

Mitchell laughed. "I would think so, after reading your book."

This seemed to surprise Evans. He grinned, his head cocked to the side, looking at Nicole with a sort of amused wonder. "You read my book?"

"How could I not? My FBI appointed therapist wrote a book about paranormal activities, including UFO abduction cases. After all the reading about abductions and sightings I did last year, I had to see what my own therapist might say about this."

"And?" Evans held out a hand.

"I hired you, didn't I?"

Evans chuckled again, shaking his head. "Maybe writing that book was worth it after all."

"What's the matter? Not a bestseller?"

"An understatement," he said. "Acknowledging how powerful the subjective experience can be for people who claim to encounter the paranormal often manages to make me some enemies on both sides. The challenge of holding a middle ground position, sometimes. One camp would like me to get my patients to as quickly as possibly dismiss these absurd superstitions, the other camp is insulted that I don't actually believe any of this paranormal hokum."

"Well, maybe this case could give you something interesting to write about next," she offered. "Who knows?"

He nodded, smiling.

"By the way," Mitchell said. "If you reach below your seat you'll find a case file."

Evans complied, bringing up the case file with the FBI insignia on it. He flipped it open on his lap and looked down at the papers. It was a thick folder with several printed reports, photos and other documents. He began leafing through it.

"That's everything we have on Tommy Ferguson," Mitchell explained. "The fourteen-year-old boy who went missing last year. For about two years he had been experiencing what he and his parents believed to be repeated alien abductions. He had only limited memories of these experiences. But they always happened at night. In the months before his disappearance, the abductions seemed to become more severe. He experienced larger periods of time he could not account for. Hours. According to his parents, he seemed perpetually on edge. He had frequent nightmares and unexplained marks on his body."

Evans listened as he continued to look through the papers. He stopped on several photographs and looked at them more closely. The first was of Tommy, just a young boy with curly hair and a bright smile. There was also a picture of a slight bulge on the back on Tommy's neck. And a third of red marks on Tommy's lower back in the form of a triangle.

"The last two times he went missing," Mitchell continued. "He was gone for more than eight hours. Once he was found about twelve miles from home, naked and incoherent. Then, April of last year he just vanished one night."

Evans looked up. "Where are his parents now?"

"Moved. They believe their son was taken by aliens, but not everyone in town is so sure. I guess they didn't feel welcome anymore. Or maybe they just needed a fresh start. Either way, they're gone. They're in Texas now."

"You've done your homework," Evans said, looking back at the files.

"I'm in contact with the local chief of police," Mitchell explained. "In Tommy's case, the FBI wasn't called in until he went missing. I'm hoping that by getting involved earlier, we can have a different outcome this time."

Evans looked over at her, considering her words, but he didn't speak. Mitchell wondered what he might be thinking, but didn't press him. He went back to the files and began reading one of the abduction reports. She let him read in silence, her mind turning to her own thoughts. Switching lanes, she buzzed around a slow car that insisted on being in the left hand lane. Time was ticking away.

THE SUN HAD DROPPED beyond the horizon, only its glow still reached across the sky. But with every passing minute, light faded and the darkness of a new night crept over the land. Long shadows morphed from mere spectators of the dying day into the true darkness of night. Having exited off of 93 North on exit 32 that led to North Woodstock or Lincoln, Mitchell consulted her phone for directions for the first time since setting out from Boston. Now, her Accord turned off the road and headed up the driveway to the Clark residence. Stopping in the circle at the end of the drive, Nicole parked the car. She looked over at Evans. "Ready to start our investigation?"

"Lead the way," he said.

They got out of the car. Looking over to the house, Mitchell saw a man in his fifties step out of the front door. He eyed them cautiously. Stopping, he crossed his arms, not leaving his porch. This must be Stephanie's father, she noted. Mitchell approached, Evans following her.

"Mr. Clark?" she said as she drew near to the steps leading up to the porch.

"Yes," Tim Clark answered. "And you might be?"

His tone wasn't exactly friendly, but this was nothing new to Mitchell. She plowed ahead, moving right up the steps to him. "I'm special agent Nicole Mitchell with the FBI." She produced her badge, showing it to Tim. "This is Dr. Alan Evans, a psychiatrist who is assisting me with this case."

Tim dropped his arms from their crossed position. His eyes bounced between Mitchell and Evans. Dorothy stepped up to the screen door and looked out, observing the exchange.

"Chief Wilson said you'd be coming. But I figured you'd be here tomorrow," Tim said.

Mitchell smiled politely. "Time is of the essence, Mr. Clark. I was hoping to speak with Stephanie."

Tim looked to his wife with weary eyes. Looking back, he gestured to the door. "Come on in."

Dorothy swung the screen door open. Mitchell and Evans entered the house. Mitchell introduced herself and Evans to Dorothy, who greeted both with more warmth than Tim. Dorothy showed them into the living room and promptly inquired if they would like any tea, coffee, water, soda, or something to eat. Mitchell turned these down, as did Evans, though she wondered if he did so only because he was following her lead. They each took a seat in one of the two individual recliners that faced the sofa. Mitchell noted the layout of the room. The television stood in the corner. It wasn't particularly large; she guessed only thirty six inches. It was not the focus of the room, but rather the two recliners and the sofa that faced each other. Between them stood a dark wood coffee table. Books sat scattered on it. By the looks of it, a couple of them were period romance novels. One was a rather thick biography of Woodrow Wilson.

Dorothy excused herself to fetch Stephanie as Mitchell and Evans took their seats. Tim stood behind the sofa and said nothing. Evans, who had a dark leather messenger bag with him, set it next to him. From it, he produced a black leather notebook and a pen. Mitchell noticed that from the notebook hung a crucifix. The thin chain of the necklace was closed in the pages of the notebook, apparently functioning as a bookmark. Evans flipped to that page. With the pen, he began making some quick notes. Mitchell wondered if this notebook must be where he kept personal notes, research, and other such things. She seldom saw him on his smartphone and wondered now also if Evans simply preferred old-fashioned things like pens and notebooks over carting around glowing screens. He had always had a legal notepad and pen during therapy, but she'd never seen this sleek black notebook during any of their sessions in his office back in Boston.

Dorothy walked back into the living room with Stephanie in tow. Both Mitchell and Evans stood and Mitchell repeated her introductions. Both Evans and Mitchell shook Stephanie's hand, but the girl's handshake was limp. Her eyes wandered between them and she seemed she might have preferred not to be bothered. Mitchell recognized the worried look in her eyes, the slouched shoulders, the dark rings under her eyes. Here was a victim.

At last, everyone took a seat. Stephanie sat between her parents on the sofa. Mitchell noted this protective arrangement. The outsiders were relegated to separate seats, the family sat snuggly together on the sofa. Dorothy, who sat to Stephanie's left, had her arm across Stephanie's back, her hand resting on Stephanie's right shoulder.

"Stephanie, I know you've been through a lot already," Mitchell began softly. "And you talked with Police Chief Wilson. But I'm hoping we can talk a little. Is that okay?"

Stephanie nodded, but she didn't make eye contact. From the corner of her eye, Mitchell watched as Evans observed Stephanie, notebook and pen at the ready.

"Can you tell me what happened last night?" Mitchell asked.

Stephanie looked down at the floor for a moment before speaking. Finally she said, "I remember I woke up in the middle of the night. Not really sure why. I just suddenly was wide awake. And ... scared."

Evans jotted something down in his notebook.

"Did you have a nightmare?" Mitchell asked.

"No. Nothing like that," Stephanie shook her head. "I don't remember having any dreams. I know I was asleep because I went to bed around a quarter to one. But the next thing I knew I was awake and it was almost three."

"What happened next?" Mitchell pressed forward.

Stephanie pursed her lips together and pushed a strand of dark hair out of her eyes. "There was this light. And my whole body went numb. Like there was this pressure all over me. It was like my whole body was suddenly cold. But it was like the cold started from here," she said, moving her hand over her heart. "I never felt so scared before. I couldn't move. It picked me up."

"It picked you up?" Mitchell glanced over at Evans who looked up from his notebook with wide eyes.

"Yeah," Stephanie nodded. "I know it sounds … It's never happened like this before."

"It's okay. After that, what happened?" said Mitchell.

Stephanie looked down at the floor again. She said nothing for a bit. Her mother and father kept their attentive eyes on her.

"Stephanie," Evans suddenly spoke up. "I know it can be really scary to talk about what happened. But we're here to help you."

"It's," Stephanie began, but paused. "I don't know. I can't really remember. There was the light. Then … " She shook her head as tears gathered in her eyes. "I was on the road and that woman was there. She seemed so scared."

Mitchell leaned in a little closer. "Focus on that light. Can you recall anything that happened after that?"

Stephanie thought for a moment, then shook her head again. "You know when you have a really bad dream and you wake up and you can't really remember what the dream was even about? But you have this feeling inside; it just stays with you for a while."

"Yeah," Mitchell said earnestly. "I know the feeling."

She could feel Evans glance over at her and figured she knew what he was thinking.

"It's like," Stephanie continued. "That's all that's left. Like they took everything else. But they leave this void … and in that void there's only fear."

"Fear?" Mitchell prompted Stephanie to continue as she seemed still slow to put into words what was in her mind.

"Yeah. Like the whole world is different somehow," Stephanie said. "Darker. Colder. Like there's something lurking behind you at every moment."

Mitchell nodded, for lack of anything better to do. This was a bleak statement for anyone to make, but to hear a nineteen-year-old say this with a sense of both familiarity and matter-of-fact detachment was chilling. Next to her, Evans quickly jotted more notes.

"I think," Stephanie carried on without prompting this time. "I think they're always watching me. And I hate it. I hate feeling like this."

"I understand," Mitchell said softly. It seemed somehow like the thing to say, but she knew it was a lie. Mitchell had never known anything like that. Solitude, loneliness, isolation? Yes. She knew those feelings well. But then, she'd never been kidnapped before.

"We're here to help you," Mitchell went on. "That's why we need you to try to remember everything you can."

Stephanie shook her head, wiping away tears from her eyes. Dorothy looked up at Mitchell with an apologetic expression. Mitchell suddenly decided on a new approach. She reached down to her own bag and retrieved a picture of Tommy. She held it out for Stephanie to see.

"Do you know this boy?" she asked.

Stephanie blinked back more tears before managing to focus on the picture. She stared at it for a moment. Her mouth dropped open slowly, her jaw seeming to go slack. Stephanie began to shake, slowly at first, but with increasing intensity. Her eyes moved past the photo, past Mitchell, and became unfocused, staring off at nothing in particular.

In a very soft voice, Stephanie suddenly spoke, "Tommy. He's with us. Tommy is with us. He's ours."

Evans, who had looked down to make more notes, looked up suddenly. Mitchell let her hand that held the photo drop without thinking about it.

"What did you say?" Mitchell asked.

Again, Stephanie spoke softly, eyes still far away, "Tommy is with us. And in three days, Stephanie will join him."

A chill ran through Mitchell. What the hell was happening to this girl? Mitchell's mind raced. Was this a sick joke? But only moments ago this same girl had been crying quietly and struggling to recall what happened to her just last night. Now this? This might be a sick joke, but Mitchell felt sure that Stephanie wasn't in on it. If anything, she was about to become the joke's twisted punch line.

"Steph? Honey?" Dorothy whispered.

Suddenly, Stephanie's eyes rolled into the back of her head, showing only white. Her head slumped to her right and her body went limp. She collapsed against her father, who immediately wrapped an arm around her.

"What happened?" Dorothy said, her voice quaking. "Stephanie?!"

Dorothy sprang to her feet, moving out of the way so Tim could gently maneuver Stephanie's now limp body onto the sofa. Laying Stephanie down, Tim turned to Mitchell.

"I think you should leave now," he said with a soft but clear voice that left no question that this was not up for discussion.

Mitchell and Evans both stood, their eyes still on the collapsed girl.

"Is she okay?" Mitchell asked.

"Check her pulse," Evans suggested.

"It's happened before," Tim explained. "She'll be fine. She just needs to rest. It's the stress. Now, please, just leave us! It's been a very long day."

"Mr. Clark, I need to see Stephanie's room," said Mitchell.

"The police have been through it already," Tim said. "Now please, leave."

Mitchell looked into the man's eyes. She nodded. Producing a business card from her suit jacket, she handed it to Tim.

"This is my cell phone number," she said. "I'm staying in town. Please call me if Stephanie remembers anything else."

He took the card, looking down at it. "And what good will that do?"

Mitchell frowned. What was this man's issue? Did he think he could protect his daughter on his own? Did he have something to hide? Did he, like Tommy's parents before him, believe that Stephanie was in fact being abducted by extraterrestrial beings?

"Mr. Clark, I don't believe in aliens," Mitchell said flatly. "I believe someone—a person—might be behind this. And if so, I'm going to stop them."

Tim's frown lightened. He nodded. "Okay."

As Mitchell walked out of the front door of the Clarks' place, headlights headed down the driveway towards them. She walked down the steps, and Evans followed behind her, his notebook still in hand. A blue pickup truck parked in the circle driveway and a man with short black hair got out. Mitchell wondered if this was a relative or family friend. The man immediately spotted them and smiled. He strode up with an ease and confidence and stuck out his hand.

"Good evening," he said in a Brazilian accent which Mitchell recognized from her exposure to her Brazilian neighbors in Somerville. "You must be the FBI agents."

Mitchell shook his hand, saying, "Actually, I'm the FBI agent, and Dr. Evans here is a consultant."

"So this is pretty serious, huh?" the man said. "Forgive me. I am Diego Silva. People here call me Pastor Diego."

"Special Agent Nicole Mitchell," she said.

Diego shook Evans's hand next, who simply gave his name as "Alan Evans," with no further credentials or explanation.

"Nice to meet you," Diego said to him. Then his eyes jumped to his notebook, and the crucifix hanging from its pages. "That's a nice crucifix."

Evans blinked then said, "Oh, this was a gift. I'm not religious."

Mitchell wondered at his answer. She'd never seen him so suddenly made uncomfortable in conversation. Something about being introduced to a man that goes by "Pastor Diego" must have prompted the reaction. She had no idea of Evans's religious affiliations or lack thereof, but then she'd only known him as her therapist and then read his book. His religious views hadn't come up in either place, but his reaction seemed a little odd, almost defensive. It was at least preemptive in its effort to establish his non-affiliation with religion. All of this flashed through Mitchell's mind, but was suddenly forgotten the moment Diego spoke.

"Good," Diego smiled. "Neither am I."

"But you're Pastor Diego?" Evans said, seeming as confused as Mitchell.

It didn't seem quite possible, but Diego's seemingly genuine grin grew bigger and he leaned forward a bit. "Ah, yes," he said. "The mystery of it! Well, I was just stopping in to check on the Clarks."

"It may not be the best time," said Mitchell. "Stephanie seems to have had some sort of episode."

The smile on Diego's face faded now. "Episode?"

"We were asking her about what happened last night. She fainted."

Diego nodded, but his eyes wandered off as he became lost in thought. "Poor girl," he mumbled.

"Does Stephanie attend your church?" Evans ventured to ask.

This brought Diego back out of his thoughts. "Her parents do. But I try to keep up with how families in our church are doing."

"And how has Stephanie been lately?" Evans continued.

"She was always a bright girl, outgoing," Diego offered. "But this past year ... things have changed for her. But she's been away at college. Hard to know exactly how she's been."

"Pastor Diego?" came Tim's voice from the house.

Diego looked up, his eyes growing bright and the smile returning. "Hi Tim. I hope it's okay if I stop by. Just wanted to see how things are going."

Tim nodded, but the slight creases on his forehead and locked jaw didn't exactly scream, come on in. Diego didn't seem bothered by this. Instead, he turned his attention back to Evans and Mitchell.

"Well, I hope you find what you are looking for," he said.

"So do I," said Mitchell.

Diego turned and headed up the steps of the house. Evans and Mitchell turned and headed to her car. They got in and Mitchell started the engine. She pulled out of the driveway and onto the road and for several minutes neither said a word. They just drove in silence, watching other cars drive by and the headlights hit the trees along the winding mountain road. Both were lost in thought, processing what they'd just experienced. Finally, Mitchell broke the silence.

"What just happened back there?" she said.

"With Stephanie?" Evans looked over at her.

"She said, 'Tommy is with us. And in three days Stephanie will join him.'"

Evans wrinkled his forehead in thought. "Could be a message from her abductors, I suppose. Or it could have some other significance."

Mitchell drummed her fingers on the steering wheel, thinking. Finally, she said, "How likely is any of that?"

"No way of knowing for sure at this point," Evans said, looking out the windshield. "But if there's any validity to what she said, I think we were just given a deadline."

He glanced over at Mitchell, who stared forward, driving.

"Three days, huh?" she said at last. "Guess we've got some work to do."

CHAPTER FIVE

SHE STILL STARED OUT the window, lost in thought. Evans looked down at his burger and wondered if he should have ordered something else. They sat in a booth at the Woodstock Station, the restaurant for the Woodstock Inn and Brewery on Main street in North Woodstock. Mitchell's chili and pint of summer seasonal beer brewed in-house sat before her untouched. Evans took a drink of his diet soda. His movement seemed to break Mitchell out of her distant stare.

"Sorry," she said. "Eat."

She took a long sip from her beer. Evans picked up his burger and began working on it. He might have mistaken Mitchell's awkwardness as relating to the fact that until recently, she had only known him as her FBI appointed therapist. But he could tell that wasn't the case. She was lost in her own world of thoughts, pouring over every syllable of the conversation they had had with Stephanie, he felt sure.

She began to work on her chili, then said, "I called ahead and booked two rooms at a motel just outside of town."

"Oh, great," Evans replied. "When did you have time to do that?"

"Before I talked to you." She grinned, eyes narrow.

"Confident I'd say yes, huh?" Evans shook his head, but smiled.

"I read your book. I knew you wouldn't turn this down," she shrugged.

Evans laughed, but wondered just how well she had him figured out. He couldn't help but feel that the tables were being turned on them. It had been his job to listen to her, observe her, and try to understand her and help her understand herself better. Now, Mitchell's investigative instincts seemed to be coming through. She'd been observing him as well all along. He just hadn't been aware of it until now.

"Right, my book," he said. "Then you know every case I've worked has conclusively indicated deep psychological issues are the root of most claims of the paranormal. And the rest are just plain misunderstandings."

"I wanted to give you a shot at a different kind of case."

He watched her return to her food, her eyes wondering back to the window, looking out past the parking lot, houses, trees, past even the mountain peaks that stood overlooking the town no matter what direction one turned.

"You're sure someone's behind this?" he prodded.

Her attention returned to him. "Healthy and well loved fourteen-year-old boys like Tommy Ferguson don't just disappear," she said. "Someone takes them. You looked through the files I gave you. Does anything in there indicate deep psychological trauma?"

"No," he admitted. "But that doesn't mean there wasn't any."

"We put that boy's parents through the ringer. They were clean."

Evans nodded and took another bite of his burger.

"So you really believe psychological trauma can explain strange lights in the sky?" Mitchell asked.

Was she testing him? Was she playing with him? Or was she honestly asking. One thing Evans was sure of was that Mitchell had careful defenses, and one of them was a rather good poker face.

"We're only starting to understand how the subconscious copes with fear, trauma, and pain," he offered.

"What about when a group of people see a UFO? What is that, a shared hallucination?"

He smiled at this, still unsure if she was testing how carefully he understood the UFO phenomena or if she was honestly curious. "It's not unheard of. It's called 'Folie à deux,' or shared psychosis. But most UFO sightings don't qualify since generally people suffering from shared psychosis have to live together in isolation. A bunch of people seeing lights over Mexico City doesn't quite fit the criteria."

"So what explains groups of people seeing UFOs?" she asked.

"Power of suggestion, for one."

"And who's making the suggestion?" She said, her eyes narrowing.

"Hard to say," Evans admitted. "There are cultural influences. There could be other factors. Often times, individuals who claim to have experiences with the paranormal have some sort of vested interest in it. So it becomes a bit of a chicken and the egg issue. Other times, people just see something they can't explain and their imaginations run wild."

"What about when people get UFOs on video?"

"Most such videos have been debunked as hoaxes or mistakes," Evans smiled. "But I guess the real question here is: what do you think?"

"Of the videos?" she asked.

"Of the UFO phenomena as a whole."

She looked away, thinking, then spoke. "I think that people desperately want to believe there's more to this life than just living on a big rock floating through space that's filled with too many people more interested in fighting over stupid superstitions than solving world hunger or finding the cure for cancer. I think, deep down, everyone wants there to be more; anything more."

She stirred her chili for a moment, looking at it. Looking up at Evans she asked, "What do you think? And don't give me some vague clinical bullshit. What do you really think?"

Evans sighed. "There's probably life out there somewhere in the universe. It's just so incomprehensibly vast. When we really consider the idea that even if our planet is the only one in our entire galaxy capable of supporting life, there are still billions of other galaxies out there. Billions upon billions. Think about it. Even if just one galaxy in one hundred million had a planet that could support life, that means there are still countless homes for life elsewhere in the universe."

Mitchell soaked this in, stirring her chili some more. Evans chuckled lightly and shook his head. "Now, whether or not life on any of those planets ever evolved to a state of intelligence is another question. But I guess it's possible. I'm not a biologist. Just a neuroscientist turned psychiatrist."

"So there has to be life out there," Mitchell pushed.

"Sure seems like it, right?" He shrugged. "But, one thing is for sure. We have never, nor will we ever, make contact with any such life forms."

"Never?" she raised her eyebrows.

"Our galaxy is something like one hundred thousand light years or more in diameter. That means all of the stars at the other end of the galaxy could blow up right now. We wouldn't know for another hundred thousand years or so. That's information traveling at the speed of light. If Einstein was right, nothing can travel faster than the speed of light. That means that unless there's life very, very close by in our galaxy—like really close—it's just impossible that they would ever be able to reach us, or us them."

Mitchell smiled, and for a brief moment he thought he saw a twinge of sadness in her eyes—or was he projecting his own feelings on her?

"Well, fuck! When you put it that way ..." She laughed. "Guess we are all alone. Even if there is life out there."

She ate more chili, thinking. "Then what explains all of these UFO stories?" she asked.

Evans considered this, then said, "I think you nailed it. We all want to believe there's more to our existence here."

"So UFOs are ... what?" she asked. "Just another form of religion?"

"For many, it occupies the same psychological and emotional space."

Mitchell frowned, seeming unsure of how to take this. Evans pushed aside his plate that still had fries on it; he suddenly didn't feel so hungry. He couldn't remember the last time he'd had a good conversation like this, particularly with a woman—though he cautioned himself on thinking along those lines too much. He leaned forward.

"Think of it this way," he said. "We cannot escape our perception of reality, so we constantly run the risk of confusing our interpretations of reality with how the universe really works. We experience things we cannot explain, and we filter them through our past experiences in order to make sense of them. For some people, when the mind is deeply traumatized, their filters become skewed. It distorts everything they experience. But the problem is that, while you and I might understand that their perception is skewed, for them, what they experience is quite true, at least on an emotive and experiential level ... a primal level, you might say."

"Makes sense," she said and ate more chili.

"You're not convinced, though." Evans sat back.

"Not yet," she admitted with a slight smirk. She looked up suddenly. "Hey, what's the deal with the crucifix?"

Evans repressed a slight laugh. Had he gotten too close to something? Why the sudden change in subject? He reminded himself that things were different now. *She's not your patient, don't treat her like one.*

"My mom gave it to me," he explained. "She raised my brother and I Catholic. Our dad wasn't around. The church meant a lot to her."

"But not to you?" she asked.

Sonofabitch, she's good, he thought. She could pick up on what his choice of words implied with a quick ease. He settled for opening up more—or did he actually want to open up more?

"It did at one point," he said. "But my mom developed early onset Alzheimer's. I watched her mind slowly fade. She became a totally different person. Towards the end, she had a good day; she remembered me. She thought I was still ten, but she knew it was me. She gave me the crucifix that she had worn every single day as long as I could remember. And she told me to always keep it with me."

Mitchell smiled warmly. "I see," she said softly.

"How about you?" Evans asked. "You've never brought up religion in our sessions."

Her warmth faded as her eyes sank back to her unfinished chili. "My religion is catching bad guys."

BLACKNESS SURROUNDED HER. SHE felt cold. Her hands reached out feeling along the metallic floor until she felt a wall. Stephanie slowly raised herself up. She stood, feeling the cold air around her. The place was pitch black. No matter where she focused her eyes, she could see nothing. Dread and panic threatened to take over her body.

A bright flash of light stunned her. She cowered against the wall. The light flashed again. She tried to look around, but the sudden intensity of the light made it nearly impossible to see anything. Her eyes couldn't quite adjust quickly enough. The light flashed again, and this time she could at least determine that it came from overhead somewhere.

A loud boom caused a scream to involuntarily leap from her throat. It was followed by metallic creaking. Then, another flash.

As the darkness returned, Stephanie spoke: "Hello?"

Another flash.

"Is there anyone there?"

She slowly moved forward, keeping her left hand on the metal wall next to her as her guide since the flashing was too disorienting. She kept moving forward without any sense that the wall changed, curved, or bent in any direction. How big was this room? Where exactly was she? But at least she seemed to slowly manage to get away from the source of the flashing so that with each subsequent flash, the intensity of the light was diminished by distance. She was starting to be able to see a little better. But the metal walls and floor were themselves black, so only the occasional seam made them noticeable at all.

She moved further, keeping her eyes focused on where she last saw a seam in the wall up ahead. When the next flash came, something stood before her! She registered the big black eyes in that brief second. She screamed! But as she did, she felt the clammy cold fingers of another being wrap themselves around her arms. There was another one behind her! She pulled with all her might against those hands, screaming. The being before her stood perfectly still, staring at her with those black eyes. She fought. But suddenly she felt her whole body go limp. It was as if they'd thrown a switch and she was no longer in control. Her heart raced. The being before her reached out to her. She wanted so desperately to scream, to fight, to run.

Stephanie jerked suddenly, waking herself at last. Cold sweat covered her body and face. She was in her own room, and her own bed. She looked around the room. The window was shut in spite of the heat. A fan ran in the corner and her alarm clock read 3:02 AM. As her mind reoriented itself, she recalled going to bed. It was a dream, right? Just a dream.

She swallowed, noticing how dry her throat felt. There was nothing to it, she needed a drink. She would much rather have stayed in bed and done all she could to go back to sleep. But now that she was aware of her thirst, it nagged at her. She tried swallowing saliva to see if she could get just enough moisture in her throat to make it bearable, but it was useless. It wasn't just her throat's dryness, it was thirst. She needed water. She threw back the thin sheet on her bed, the only covering she could manage in the heat, and headed for the bathroom.

Once in the bathroom, she found a glass she'd left there for exactly such occasions and filled it up in the sink. Bringing it up to her lips, she drank deeply, surprised at just how thirsty she had been. But as she drank, a long creaking sound from somewhere in the house caught her attention. She paused mid drink. Her eyes locked on the bathroom door she'd left partially open. There was only blackness beyond it.

Lowering the still half full glass of water, she kept her eyes locked on the partially open door. Another long creaking sound travelled through the house. Was someone up? Certainly someone must be awake. But as much as she tried to convince herself that there was a reasonable explanation for the creaking, something about the quality of the sound, how long each creak lasted, stirred panic within her. She could feel a chill in her chest as her heart raced.

She moved forward quickly, putting out her hand to push the bathroom door closed. As she did so, a hand reached out and stopped the door. Instinctively, Stephanie screamed at the hand. But as the scream escaped her mouth, she realized the hand belonged to her father, who stood just outside the door.

Tim pushed the door open, an expression of confusion and shock on his face. "Stephanie! What's the matter?" he demanded.

"Dad!" was all she could manage at first. "You scared the shit out of me!"

"Hey. Language," he reprimanded her.

Embarrassed and now angry, Stephanie set the glass aside and pushed past her father and headed back to her room. She climbed back in her bed and tried to calm herself. It would be a while now before she could fall back to sleep. Her heart still thumped hard inside her chest. Her breathing was shallow. First the nightmare, now this. The night was a waste.

She closed her eyes, trying to force herself to calm down, but the darkness felt somehow oppressive and she couldn't keep them closed for long. She looked about the room. Through her closed door and walls, she heard the toilet flush in the bathroom followed by the sink running. At last, the sound of her father walking back to his room could be heard. Once he was back in bed, the house returned to silence. The small fan in her room droned on, providing a bed of constant noise.

She looked at the window. Thoughts of the dream she had just had threatened to take over her mind. She needed something else to focus on, anything else. She reached for her smartphone, but then retracted her hand. She'd never get to sleep this way. She needed to sleep. Tomorrow—well, today, actually—was Monday. She was back on duty as a life guard at one of the resorts in Lincoln. It wasn't much of a job, but it was close to home and managed to help her earn some money before heading back to college in the fall.

She rolled over in her bed, facing away from the window. Again, she closed her eyes, trying to still her rushing mind. She focused on slowing her breathing and trying to consciously relax. Slowly, her mind cleared. Feeling relaxation set in, she felt hopeful that soon she might fall back asleep. She needed it; being a lifeguard could be quite tedious. Being a lifeguard running on little sleep meant she would be tempted to fall asleep at some point in the afternoon heat. That was definitely not an option.

As her mind began to drift in the aimless ways it did just before at last being overtaken by slumber, the image of the grey figure with large black eyes standing before her popped into her brain. She opened her eyes suddenly as a reflex. She was still in her room. But now, something felt different. A chill climbed up her back, the hair on her arms standing up. She felt sure something stood behind her, looking at her.

She tried to convince herself she was still upset by the dream. But then, she heard the slight tapping sound! And she knew it was there.

She didn't need to turn. She knew it was in the room with her. Her breathing came in short gasps now. What choice did she have? Ignoring them never sent them away.

Stephanie whirled around in time to catch a glimpse of a silhouetted figure moving in front of the window and into the corner with her mirror. She had only a second to take in the moving slender frame, the large head, and lanky arms. She screamed, knowing it lurked in the shadows just out of sight.

From the hallway, she heard the commotion of her father and mother rushing to her room. Her door flew open and the lights came on. And in the light she saw ... nothing.

The mirror stood in the corner as it always did, and there was no being there. There was no place it could have gone, but it wasn't there. She was absolutely positive she'd seen it. But where was it now?

"What is it, sweetie?" her mother asked. "What happened?"

Stephanie turned and flung her face into her pillow. All her pent-up fear rushed out of her lungs as she sobbed. It was as if her body reacted of its own will to the vile poison that was all that fear rushing through her. She muffled her cries in her pillow. She could feel her mother and father sit down on the bed on either side of her, but she couldn't stop herself from crying.

"Steph," her mother said, "Everything's okay. It was only a dream. You're safe."

No. No, she wasn't safe! She was sure of that now. She fought the sobbing, trying to form words. All that came out was, "No! No!"

She fought harder against the emotions, struggling to breathe. Pushing herself away from her pillow, she at last managed to spit out, "No. I'm not safe!" She fought against the dizziness that threatened to overrun her consciousness. "It was here! It was in the room!"

CHAPTER SIX

THE RINGING OF HER cell phone had pulled Mitchell out of the dream she must have been having that morning. The dream evaporated instantly, leaving only a slight sense of heaviness, of regret. Her eyes had opened and she had tried to focus on the world around her. For a second everything seemed off until the memory of where she was came to her. She had reached over and picked up her smartphone, unplugging it from the charger cord that ran to the outlet on the lamp that sat on the bedside table. The call had been from the North Woodstock police station. Now driving down the road in her car with Evans in the passenger seat, she felt more awake. The heaviness of her dream slowly evaporated.

Next to her, Evans yawned. She had called him immediately after hanging up with Officer O'Conner. Then she'd quickly jumped in the shower. He appeared to have done the same, but still struggled to seem alert.

"So, what time did this happen?" Evans asked her.

She'd only given him minimal information so far. "According to Officer O'Conner, just after 3:00 AM. Stephanie claimed someone was in the room with her. Her parents found no evidence anyone was there."

Evans looked out the window as they came upon an intersection. "Don't we turn there to go to the Clark's house?" he pointed.

"We're not going to their house," Mitchell said as she maintained speed.

She proceeded to fill him in on the details of whatever had happened to Stephanie last night had been relayed to her over the phone as they drove. They had a ways to go yet. Apparently Stephanie had dreamed, woken up, and then claimed to have seen someone or something in her room.

"But how do we know it wasn't all a bad dream?" Evans asked.

"That's what I'm hoping you can help determine" Mitchell smiled at him.

"You still haven't told me where we're going," he pointed out.

"St. Jerome," she answered.

"Hospital?" Evans said, looking off and searching his mind for any recollection of such a place.

"It's an old mental ward," she said.

He looked over at her, frowning. "Oh," he said softly. "They think she's crazy." He shook his head, looking out his window.

They drove on in silence.

FORTY-FIVE MINUTES LATER, MITCHELL'S car pulled into the long driveway leading up a hill to the large three story brick building. Its windows were all dark, and as they approached, they could see that bars covered them. The driveway wound up the hill and led to a parking lot.

Only a few cars sat scattered in the lot. Large stone steps led up to the archway entrance of the building. It appeared more gothic with every yard that they approached.

At last, Mitchell parked the car and they walked to the steps leading up to the main doors. Over the archway were engraved the words, "St. Jerome Mental Ward." They both looked up at the words as they walked in. Evans, out of polite instincts, reached the door first and held it open for Mitchell. She entered and he followed her.

The waiting area seemed paused in time. Old chairs sat arranged around a large rug. They all were likely brand new sometime in the early 1970's. The chairs were boxy wood frames with orange upholstering. A desk sat by the wall, on it was an old CRT computer monitor. A man sat there in nursing uniform, looking over a clipboard full of papers. Mitchell headed for him without hesitation and Evans followed.

Reaching the desk, Mitchell wasted no time. She pulled out her badge and said, "Good morning, I'm Special Agent Nicole Mitchell. I understand Stephanie Clark was brought in here."

The nurse looked up from his papers. For a second he just stared at the badge. Evans had to figure this was the first time a bona fide FBI agent had walked up to this man and introduced herself in such an official manner. The man snapped out of it and nodded.

"Doctor Jeffries is just wrapping up with the family," he said.

He pointed down a hallway to their right. The hallway was long, stretching off the length of the building. About halfway down the hall a doctor stood with Tim and Dorothy Clark. They spoke, the doctor shaking his head now and again, gesturing with his hands, palms up. Evans recognized the body language as that of someone either guarded or not optimistic.

Without another word, Mitchell started walking down the hallway towards the Clarks and the doctor. Evans followed, but he made no effort to catch up to her. He didn't feel comfortable interrupting the mother and father as the doctor talked to them. Mitchell, on the other hand, seemed to feel there were more pressing matters at hand. But as she approached, the conversation between the doctor and the Clarks seemed to wrap up. The Clarks looked up at the approaching FBI agent.

"Mr. and Mrs. Clark, how is Stephanie?" Mitchell asked as she reached them.

"I'm sorry, who are you?" the doctor asked, his already wrinkled forehead becoming more wrinkled with the raising of his eyebrows.

Mitchell repeated her official greeting, badge out. The doc nodded, but before he could say anything else, Dorothy Clark jumped in.

"She's sedated right now" Dorothy said. "She was in hysterics."

Tim looked at his wife through narrow eyes. Was he unhappy with Dorothy's easy willingness to divulge information to Mitchell? Evans watched him as his eyes moved from Dorothy to Mitchell. They seemed to be in a perpetual squint. His lips firmly together, jaw set. But he made no move of protest, no indication he would rather his wife not speak.

"What exactly happened?" said Mitchell.

"She said," Dorothy hesitated, thinking. "She saw someone in her room. I'm sure it was just a nightmare. But Tim thought it would be best if we brought her in for some professional help."

Dorothy glanced over at the doctor. Tim's eyes dropped to the floor. Evans tried to track all of this. Meanwhile, Mitchell pressed on.

"It's probably for the best," she said. "She will be safer here."

At this, Tim looked up at Mitchell, his eyes wider now. Surprise? Relief? Evans wasn't sure. But his expression was certainly softer. It was clear to Evans that whether Mitchell believed it or not, she'd said the right thing to build a little trust with Tim.

"I would like to look over Stephanie's room," Mitchell continued.

This brought back the squint to Tim's eyes. "Why is that?" he asked.

"We have to cover all of our bases, Mr. Clark," Mitchell explained. "What if Stephanie is telling the truth? What if someone was there last night? This kidnapper's pattern is to abduct his victims multiple times. So we have to seriously consider the possibility that someone was, in fact, in Stephanie's room last night. And if so, maybe they left some evidence."

Tim's squint moved over to his wife. She shot him a pleading look. Evans figured this meant there must be some kind of ideological divide between the two, at least on this matter. Tim was the one that had insisted Stephanie be brought in to a mental ward in the middle of the night. Dorothy, on the other hand, seemed ready to comply with anything Mitchell asked of them. Possibly she did not think her daughter was mentally ill or suffering some sort of emotional or psychological breakdown. Either way, Tim seemed to relent at her look. He glanced at Mitchell, nodding.

"Thank you," Mitchell said, sincerity in her voice. "We'll head right over."

Evans frowned. They'd driven all this way to have this conversation? She didn't want see Stephanie? Granted, the girl was sedated. But it seemed like so little for such a long drive. Maybe she felt this could not have been done over the phone. Or maybe he was missing something. Either way, Evans felt the need to jump in.

"Pardon me," he said.

Suddenly all eyes were on him. Evans pulled out a business card and handed it to the doctor.

"I'm Dr. Alan Evans. I'm working with the FBI. Would you please make sure that everyone working today knows that when Stephanie wakes up, I would like a phone call. It's important."

The doctor looked down at Evans's card. "She'll be out for a while, but we'll be sure to call when she wakes."

"Thank you," Evans said.

THEY STEPPED OUT INTO the hot summer air. Mitchell walked down the steps, thoughts rushing through her mind. Stephanie had claimed someone was at her place and now she was in a mental ward, sedated no less. It was clear now what her father's view of the situation was. Or was he in some strange way trying to save face? Obviously he was well aware of what had happened to the Ferguson family only a year ago.

"Does it strike you as noteworthy that Stephanie's father felt it important to bring her here?" Evans asked her as they walked down the steps. He clearly was thinking along the same lines.

"I guess we know what he thinks is going on here," she said.

"Do we, though?" Evans raised his eyebrows.

They reached the end of the stairs and continued walking to the car.

"All we know for sure," Evans said, "is that Mr. Clark might at least prefer having what appears to be a mentally ill daughter than one being abducted by UFOs. But what if there's more to his motivations?"

Mitchell looked over at Evans as they walked. "You think it's suspicious?" she asked.

"I don't know. But I think he might be right about one thing: Stephanie is disturbed. But the source of her distress may not be a kidnapper or aliens."

"Her father?" Mitchell said.

"Just a theory," Evans shrugged.

Mitchell looked off, mulling this over.

"You don't agree?" Evans asked.

She stopped by her car and turned to Evans. "Are you coming

around to my way of thinking? Someone's behind this?"

"Well, not exactly," Evans said.

"Why kidnap her and drop her off in the middle of nowhere?"

"I didn't say he was alone in this, or that he's even the one doing this. Look, I'm still not convinced that there is an actual kidnapper behind Stephanie's abductions. All I'm saying is that, if there is a kidnapper, then her father may be complicit." Evans paused for a moment, then finished by saying, "Which is why you're not going to find anything in her room."

He opened the door to the car and got in. Mitchell grinned. Is he starting to get an attitude? Or is he playing with me? She watched him as he clicked his seatbelt into place. He looked back out at her through the car window.

"Oh, come on. Don't look so disappointed," he said, his voice muffled by the car.

She grinned, walking around the front of the car to the driver's side. She climbed in and started the car. As she buckled her seatbelt, she said, "Well, I guess we'll just have to go see if there really is nothing to find, won't we?"

"I guess so," Evans grinned.

Mitchell pulled out her phone and placed a call before throwing the car into drive and pulling out of the parking lot. As she drove down the long driveway back to the road, she brought the phone up to her ear.

"Chief Wilson," she said into the phone. "It's Agent Mitchell. I was wondering if I could borrow Officer O'Conner."

MITCHELL'S FLASHLIGHT SWEPT ACROSS the dusty floor underneath Stephanie's bed. She laid on her side as she peered under the bed. She found a few pairs of shoes and a few crumpled receipts. But nothing seemed out of order. And judging from the thin layer of dust that remained undisturbed, nothing had moved in the last few days.

Mitchell sighed, reaching out her hand, Evans took it and helped her back to her feet. By the window, Officer O'Conner inspected the window frame closely. She moved to the lock and shined her own flashlight on it even though sunlight from outside poured through the window. O'Conner squinted as she moved her head around, carefully taking in if any marks had been made recently to the old window lock.

They had been over the room carefully. Nothing at all seemed out of place as far as Mitchell could tell. They had asked the Clarks a series of questions about how Stephanie had been the previous night. Everything pointed to a vivid nightmare, Mitchell hated to admit.

"Fine. It looks like you might be right," Mitchell admitted. "There's just nothing here. So what? I owe you a beer?"

Evans shrugged and smiled. "I got lucky."

"No, that's more than luck," Mitchell shook her head. "What are you thinking?"

"Well, chances are Stephanie is suffering from some form of PTSD that manifests itself in nightmares and even waking dreams. She probably did see something here in her room last night. It just might not have actually been here."

He pulled out his notebook with the crucifix and flipped through the pages until he landed where the chain marked his spot. He began making notes.

"Right," Mitchell said, "But something has to have caused that PTSD."

Officer O'Conner shrugged and turned from the window. "No evidence of forced entry and the Clarks assure me this window was locked last night. The whole house was locked up," she said. But then in a softer voice, she added, "But then, that's never stopped them before."

Mitchell's attention shifted completely to O'Conner. She'd met her a year ago, but they had spent limited time together. She recalled that O'Conner had a fiancé at the time. She realized that in her focus on the case, she hadn't even asked about how she was doing. Glancing down at her hand, she noticed the wedding band on her left hand. But what really drew in Mitchell's attention was that last statement. Could it be that O'Conner was a believer?

"Them?" Mitchell asked.

"The ..." O'Conner pointed up, "you know ... aliens."

Evans looked up from his notebook now and Mitchell could see the hint of bemusement in his eyes and in the way the right corner of his lip curled up ever so slightly.

"You believe in aliens, officer?" He asked.

O'Conner looked from Evans back to Mitchell, possibly regretting having brought the subject up. "Now I know what you're thinking, but I'm no gullible yokel. I believe in what I can see. And for a long time, I thought all this talk about UFOs was absurd."

Mitchell wondered how long ago her mind had changed. Had it been after the Tommy Ferguson case or maybe during?

"But ..." Evans prompted her.

"But then I saw something," O'Conner said, her voice low but with no hesitation. "About a year and half ago, I was on a speed trap. From where I parked, I could see Linden Pond. Must have been about two hours into my shift there, I saw lights in the sky out over the pond. There were three orbs of light. One came down and silently went into the pond. The other two circled around and around. The next morning, we got a call from Frank Simmons. He's got a farm about a mile away from there. One of his cows had been killed, drained of every last drop of blood and cut up. Local vet didn't know what to make of it. The cuts were made with surgical precision. Several organs were missing, including the genitals."

Evans nodded.

"So this was before the Ferguson case?" Mitchell asked.

"Yes. I believe you read about it in our files," O'Conner said.

"I don't recall you seeing lights, though."

"I never filed an official report. But there was a report made about Frank's mutilated cow," O'Conner explained.

"I see," Mitchell said.

"If you're wondering," O'Conner continued. "I didn't come to really believe there might be anything to all this UFO business until after we investigated the Ferguson case. As a matter of fact, the last few years, there've been a lot of cases of lights in the sky and other such strangeness."

"And people report them to the police?" Evans asked.

"Sure they do," O'Conner replied. "Not every time, and not always officially, but most folk want to talk to us about anything suspicious so we can keep an eye out for it too. These are our friends and neighbors, after all."

"Is there any chance we could take a look at your files on those cases?" Evans said.

LOCATED ON LOST RIVER Road, the North Woodstock Police Station was a small single story building with white vinyl siding. Inside, in one of the small rooms used for meetings and the occasional interrogation, Mitchell sat at the table. She checked her phone, seeing she'd missed a call from Anthony. He was probably checking into how things were going. She'd call him back later.

Officer O'Conner walked into the room with a large file box. She set it on the table.

"This is every case we've had in the last six years," she said.

"Thank you," Mitchell said as she stood and looked down at the box.

O'Conner turned to head for the door.

"Officer O'Conner," Mitchell said, turning to her. "It's good to see you again."

O'Conner stopped at the door, looking back. "Likewise," she said. "I was sorry to hear about your partner."

Mitchell just nodded.

"You need anything else, you just call," O'Conner continued—for which Mitchell was glad. "I've been through all of these files myself trying to make sense of just what the hell is happening around here. So, if you have any questions, I'm happy to help."

"Thank you," Mitchell said.

"Hopefully things turn out differently this time," O'Conner said before turning to head out the door.

Mitchell turned back to the box on the table and stared down at it. It was, in fact, a pretty full box. What the hell is going on around here? She reached into the box and pulled out one of the folders. She sat back down and began looking through the files inside the folder.

Evans walked in a moment later with two cups of coffee. He set one down on the table near Mitchell then took a seat across from her.

"Thanks," Mitchell said, not looking up from the case file. "Where do you want to start? I'm familiar with most of these since last year Jeff and I ..."

She drifted off. At the sound of her own voice saying her partner's name out loud, it was as if a vice had suddenly squeezed her heart. Just a year ago, they had been in this same room, pouring over many of the same case files. Now he was gone. She stared down at the case files, but her eyes were unfocused.

"You okay?" Evans asked, looking around the file box between them.

"Yeah," Mitchell shook herself out of it. "I'm fine. Let's get to work."

She laid the file out on the table and began explaining to Evans. "This one is just some lights seen hovering out near Paradise Road. It later appeared over Pemigewasset River that cuts right through town."

"How about you tell me what you know, and we'll take it from there," Evans offered.

Mitchell closed the folder before her and grabbed another one. "This one's someone claiming they saw a UFO on their street and then shortly thereafter, Big Foot came out and waved."

"You serious?" Evans chuckled.

"Well, not about the waving part," Mitchell smiled.

She set that folder aside as well and then pulled out the next. This proceeded for a while. She paused and opened folders and read enough to jog her memory before giving Evans a quick summary. Sometimes he would have questions, other times they would just move on. They spent a good while discussing the case of a local drunk who'd claimed to have been abducted. Evans also took particular interest in the case of some tourists who had stayed in town and gone hiking in nearby Lost River Canyon. One had gone missing for two days. The other two claimed a UFO had abducted the man. He turned up later, but the consensus seemed to be that all three had been stoned out of their minds while hiking. As this went on, they drained their coffee cups.

One case involved a detailed explanation by a local woman in her fifties who claimed to have been taken aboard a ship and examined about three years ago. It fit the UFO abduction scenario. Evans even remarked that it seemed to fit it too neatly. Almost any of the details, the saucer ship, the lights, the grey beings, the examination, the missing time, the telepathic communication, could have been lifted from any number of other UFO stories—actually reported or in TV shows and movies. Either this woman was describing a genuine experience many others shared or the suggestions of such an event were so strong that familiarity with UFO folklore filled in the generic details, he pointed out.

Finally, they reached case files that were new to Mitchell. They opted to divide them and they both began to read. After a bit, however, Evans stood and announced it was time to return the borrowed coffee. He headed out of the room. Mitchell poured over a case file that told of another mutilation of local livestock. This time it was a goat, but the details were similar: the goat had several internal organs taken. There was no blood at the scene of the crime. However, marks on the animal's neck indicated where blood might have been drained from the goat. What's next? Mitchell wondered. Did the Chupacabra decide to visit the White Mountains? I mean, I guess everyone needs a vacation. She grinned, imagining a tabloid article titled, "Chupacabra Seen Skiing the White Mountains.

She set the file aside and grabbed another. This new one appeared to be about a local resident seeing alien beings on his property. As Mitchell began to read, Evans walked back into the room. Mitchell's jaw dropped as she read the details of the case. Evans noticed this and stopped where he stood.

"What is it?" he asked.

"It's a report from last year," Mitchell said.

"About Tommy's case?"

She looked up at Evans. "I think we need to go pay Pastor Diego a visit."

CHAPTER SEVEN

Nestled behind the brewery and restaurant in North Woodstock stood a small old church building. Its steeple that housed a bell had a cross on its top that reached up to the sky. Its white siding contrasted with the red doors to the church. Beyond it, trees swayed in the growing summer breeze. Clouds rolled in over the tree covered mountains that surrounded the town. The air felt heavier and more humid. A storm was coming. Mitchell's Accord pulled into the paved parking lot to the church that separated it from the deep red building of the brewery just to its right. Pastor Diego's blue pickup truck sat next to the church building.

Mitchell got out of the car, looking around. The street curved just after the church and headed off into a small residential area. Everything was quiet. Mitchell couldn't help but wonder if living in a place like this would ultimately be peaceful for her or unsettling. Would she get restless and miss life in the city? It was so much quieter. At the moment, it felt welcoming and soothing. But would she eventually be aggravated by the quiet?

"I guess he's in, huh?" Evans said, as he got out of the car and looked over at Diego's truck. "I thought pastors took Mondays off since they work Sunday."

"According to Officer O'Conner, he's here pretty much all the time," Mitchell said.

They walked up to the front door. Mitchell tried it but found it locked. They headed around the side of the building and tried the red door that faced the parking lot. That one they found open. Stepping in, they found the place quiet with few lights on. The side door and the front door both lead into a small foyer which gave way to the small sanctuary. Though the walls were white, with no lights on, the place was dim. The stained glass windows limited the amount of sunlight that could come in, and as more clouds rolled in, the mid-day sun became occluded.

Mitchell proceeded to the entrance to the sanctuary and looked around. Rows of wooden pews led to the front of the church where a simple podium stood. Behind it were two rows meant for a small choir and an ornate table with the words, "In Memory of Me." A large stained glass window overlooked the sanctuary from the front, displaying an artist's rendition of Jesus praying over a rock.

"An interesting choice," Evans remarked.

Mitchell looked over at him and saw that he too was taking in the sight of the stained glass window. They stopped at the front of the sanctuary and looked up at the glowing glass portrait.

"Why is that?" she asked.

"Jesus in the Garden of Gethsemane, praying," Evans explained. "Suffering really. He knows he's about to be betrayed by Judas, tortured, and then crucified. Most protestant churches stick to a clean cross with no suffering Jesus hanging from it. This church, however, didn't go for that."

"It's been here a long time," Pastor Diego's voice echoed in the empty sanctuary.

They turned to see that he now stood at the back of the sanctuary. He smiled and walked towards them.

"I merely inherited this place when I was given this post," he said.

"Given this post?" Mitchell said. "You make it sound like a military assignment."

Diego grinned and nodded. "Maybe it is."

"That's also an interesting bit of decor," Evans pointed out, gesturing to a small wooden table that sat off to the left side of the podium.

Mitchell hadn't noticed it until now. She glanced over and saw that on the table stood several pictures in frames of people, including a picture of Stephanie. Now that is interesting!

"They're reminders for our congregation to pray," Diego said. "I mean, everyone has something they could use prayer for. But these people in particular need every prayer we can manage."

Mitchell turned back to Diego and said, "Pastor Diego, we'd like to talk. Do you have a moment?"

Diego indicated the front pew to his right. "Please, have a seat. How may I help the FBI?"

Evans and Mitchell moved to the pew and sat down. Diego quickly fetched a folding chair from a short stack of such chairs that sat leaning against the wall near the front pew. He unfolded it and set it so he could face the two of them and took a seat.

Wasting no further time, Mitchell dove in. "About a year ago, you called the police to report an incident."

"Yes," Diego nodded.

"What was that incident, exactly?" she asked.

Diego looked down at the floor, thinking. He sighed then said, "I was asleep in my house. I woke up. I'm not sure why I woke up. I'm usually a very heavy sleeper. But that night, I woke up around three in the morning. And I was just ... uncomfortable. No ... uneasy. So I got up and went downstairs. That's when I smelled something."

"What's that?" Mitchell said.

"Sulfur," Diego stated. "I thought I had some kind of leak in the house, so I checked the kitchen. That's when I saw lights in the field. So I walked outside and I saw them. They were standing maybe fifty meters away, close to the fence. There were lights and these ... beings."

"Aliens?" Mitchell asked.

From the corner of her eye, Mitchell could see Evans look over at her, his mouth open as if to say something—probably to protest her leading question. But Diego was too quick with his answer.

"Yes," he said. "I guess."

"What did they do?" she carried on with the interrogation.

"They just stood there and stared at me with those ... big black eyes ... soulless eyes," Diego said, looking off, lost in the memory. His words came slowly, his voice soft. "They never came any closer, and I didn't approach them. After a bit, they vanished into their bright lights and the lights shot into the sky. I thought I'd been out there for only a few minutes. But when I got back into the house, I saw the clock on the stove said 3:42 AM. I was out there for almost forty minutes."

"In the police report, it says you didn't call the police until two days after this happened. Why?" Mitchell asked.

Diego licked his lips and looked down. "That night I saw those things ... That was the same time that boy, Tommy Ferguson, went missing."

Evans's eyes grew wide and he glanced at Mitchell. She, however, continued to look right at Diego. She'd instantly recognized the date in the report, but she had wondered if Diego would admit to this connection.

"What made you call the police when you did?" she asked him.

"I knew the Fergusons," Diego explained. "They occasionally came to our church. When I heard that their boy was missing, I forgot all about this, until ... they told me about Tommy's experiences. That's when I realized that I probably should speak to the police in case there was in fact some connection."

Mitchell nodded, then said, "Pastor Diego, where are you from?"

"Brazil."

"How long have you been here?"

"In the States? Eight years. But in New Hampshire, only three."

"You don't seem like the usual small town pastor. What brought you here?"

At this, Diego smiled. "You might say I was called."

"Do you say you're called?" Mitchell continued the interrogation.

"I believe and hope there is a reason."

Mitchell looked over at Evans now, giving him a slight nod to indicate that if he had any questions he should go ahead and ask them. She felt almost as if she might as well have said, "your witness." Evans picked up on this and dove in.

"Pastor Diego," he began, "what do you believe you saw that night?"

"You mean, do I believe in aliens?" Diego cut right to the heart of the question.

"Sure," Evans said.

Diego's eyes seemed distant and heavy to Mitchell. Yet he smiled slightly. It struck her as a knowing smile that masked secrets and hidden pain. What exactly was this man's story? Why was he here?

"I believe God is infinite," Diego said. "That creating is so part of God it must be like breathing for us. Might God have made other races on other planets? Maybe ... probably."

Evans raised his eyebrows and nodded slightly. Mitchell wondered if this was what he had expected Diego to say. Her experiences with religious types left her with the impression that generally pastors and clergy had a distinctly egocentric view of humanity. Human beings were created in the image of God and thus the pinnacle of all creation. And given that the Bible didn't directly address life on other planets, this seemed a good enough reason for many religious people to dismiss the notion that God might have made life elsewhere in the universe. Of course, the Bible also didn't directly address black holes or quantum particles, as an ex-boyfriend of hers had pointed out during a lively discussion at a holiday party with a religious guy he had worked with at the time.

"But," Diego spoke slowly, looking at Evans, "you're asking me if what I believe I saw that night were aliens."

Diego leaned forward in his chair, which creaked. He looked from Evans to Mitchell, then back before speaking.

"I'm a man of faith, Dr. Evans. Maybe that makes me biased, or maybe it makes me particularly sensitive to certain things. What I encountered that night was not of this world."

"Why do you say that?" Evans asked.

"Because the entire time I looked at them," Diego said, his eyes locked now on Evans. "I could feel their hatred. They were surrounded in light, but it was as if they were ... sucking all hope and joy right out of me. I've experienced many things in my life. But that night, I looked evil in the eyes. And it looked back at me ... and it knew me."

Evans simply stared back at Diego, possibly unsure of how to respond. A slight chill ran up Mitchell's spine at Diego's words. But she told herself he was being over dramatic. Evil is not a person that it might know anyone, she reminded herself. Things were getting off track, and ultimately none of this superstitious bullshit would actually resolve anything. It was time to go.

"Thank you for your time, Pastor Diego," she said and stood.

Evans, whether done or not followed her. As she walked down the center isle of the sanctuary, she heard the creaking of Diego's chair as he stood.

"You know," Diego said, louder now so he could be heard, his voice echoing off the high wood ceiling. "since that night ..."

Mitchell stopped, looking back. Evans did so as well.

"I wake up almost every night around 3:00 AM," Diego continued. "It has become my private prayer vigil for people like Tommy and Stephanie."

Mitchell nodded, unsure what she might be expected to say to this. Turning, she headed into the foyer and out the side door. She'd had enough of that place for one day.

EVANS WALKED OUTSIDE, FINDING that Mitchell was already behind the wheel of her car. She'd gone after Pastor Diego unapologetically. But then he wondered if this was simply how every interrogation was handled. He walked to the passenger side and got in. Mitchell wasted no time.

"What do you think?" she asked.

"Well," Evans stalled, trying to gather his thoughts. "He seems sincere."

"Yeah," she said halfheartedly. "He does, doesn't he? Hmmm."

Evans eyed her carefully. "You think he's a suspect."

"Suspect might be too strong of a word. Let's just say suspicious."

She started the car and put it into reverse, backing out of the parking spot. She pulled out into the street and took a left, heading to Main Street.

"Where to now?" Evans asked.

"I want to see the spot where Stephanie was found," she answered.

She took a left onto Main Street and headed out of town. As they drove, the wind picked up, darker clouds rolling in. Evans looked out at the sky and wondered when Mitchell might slow down. They had skipped lunch in their digging through the files and then going to talk to Diego. And now they were headed to yet another location. But he sensed Mitchell's drive, her urgency. All the same, he was growing quite hungry. They drove for a bit in silence, both lost in thought. He ran back through what Diego had said.

The man seemed sincere enough, but Evans wondered about his story of seeing alien beings. Was there anyone in this town that didn't believe in aliens or hadn't seen a UFO? But he reminded himself that just because O'Conner and now Pastor Diego seemed to think there might be something to all of this that didn't mean the whole town shared such experiences and beliefs. It was just a lot to take in so quickly.

Eventually they reached a spot where Mitchell pulled over, but Evans, lost in thought, hadn't tracked where exactly they were now. Mitchell looked down at her phone where she had a map pulled up. She had marked a spot on the map. She closed the app and looked up at him.

"We're here," she said. "I guess."

Opening her door, she got out of the car. Evans followed her, starting to understand why she was single. On the one hand, he admired her tenacity. On the other hand ... he was hungry.

Mitchell walked up the road a bit then stopped to look at tire marks in the road. "So the woman was coming from that direction," she pointed up the road. "... saw Stephanie in the road here, and slammed on her breaks." She looked back in the opposite direction. "So where did Stephanie come from?"

"Hard to say," Evans replied. "She could have been walking on the road for a while or just have come out of the woods."

He looked around. The road cut through the woods. There were trees going on endlessly lining the road from either side. There was no way of really knowing where Stephanie might have come from.

Mitchell headed to the side of the road and then walked into the woods. Evans followed her to the edge of the road and then looked out at the woods. I hope the FBI pays their consultants well, he thought, looking down at his shoes. I probably should have negotiated my fee first. He followed her into the woods.

"Might I remind you that it's tick season?" He called after her.

"Don't worry, I can check you for ticks later," she called back to him.

He was taken aback as he tried to determine if this was simple humor or if there was some other undercurrent of flirtation or innuendo meant to be associated with this remark. He opted to just move on.

"What do you expect to find out here?" he said.

Mitchell stopped, looking around at the vegetation around her. "Any indication she might have come through here," she said. "And what direction she came from."

She stooped and looked at the ground closely. Evans caught up to her.

"Was there any mud or leaves on her clothes?" he asked.

"Not according to the report. But her clothes were on inside-out," she said, standing back up. "I've noticed that's common in UFO abduction cases. Why is that?"

"Well, from what I've read, it's because subjects are stripped for examination. Presumably, in the process, the aliens peel their clothes off, which end up being inside-out. Then they put the inside-out clothing back on the people before returning them."

"So these beings that travelled here from some other galaxy don't know how to deal with clothing?" Mitchell frowned.

"Well, in their defense, in most abduction accounts they're usually naked themselves, or maybe it's deliberate. When you consider just what is involved in most alien abduction accounts, it's like everything they do is designed to inflict the maximum amount of terror and humiliation."

Mitchell turned and moved further into the woods, looking about. "Designed, huh? Coming around to my theory that there's someone behind this?" She remarked.

"I still strongly suspect emotional trauma as the real issue. But I have to admit that there is something quite perverse about abduction stories," he said, moving after her.

"Snatching people out of their beds at night is pretty perverse."

"That's the tame part. Abductees claim to be subjected to humiliating medical examinations. These aliens seem keenly interested in human sexuality and reproduction. There are many stories of alien beings having sex with human abductees. There's a particularly famous case of a Brazilian farmer who was abducted and then made to mate with a strange alien woman. There's plenty of other stories of sexual encounters with aliens too. But it all seems a little unnecessary since other stories claim that eggs are extracted from women and semen extracted from men."

"Ugh," Mitchell said, turning to face him with an amused look. "Alien happy ending?"

"Pass," Evans grinned. "But it does bring up the question: why bother with sex if they can extract the genetic material they need by other methods? Unless, of course, the sex is the point in those cases."

"What do you mean?"

"Well, everything about the abduction experience seems designed to be cold, horrifying, and degrading. Darkness, paralyses, nakedness, metal examination tables, sharp utensils, and this strange focus they have on sexuality."

"So they're interstellar perverts?" Mitchell shook her head.

"At least that's the modern mythology we've created," Evans said.

"Mythology?" Mitchell raised an eyebrow.

"In ancient Greece, we had the gods and goddesses, and heroes—half god, half human—brought about by sexual relations between gods and humans. There were supposedly good gods like Zeus and mischievous gods like Hermes. In medieval times, we had goblins, trolls, demons, succubus—all kinds of horrors. In fact, alien abduction stories share many similarities to the succubus narrative. Both come at night while we sleep, cause paralysis, have a sexual interest in their victims, and cause a lot of terror."

"So then we're after a succubus now?" she said.

"All of these things have served as a means to make our fear of the unknown tangible," Evans tried to explain. "Our minds constantly work to assimilate information that will help keep us alive. It is, in fact, what our brains are hardwired to do. There's good evidence in neuroscience that our brains have evolved specifically to glean as much survival information as possible from every situation. In fact, this may well be why storytelling is such a natural draw to us. The human brain latches on to the narrative and empathizes with the characters as a means to glean valuable survival information should it ever find itself in a similar predicament. And stories commonly serve as a means to make sense of our fears—thus the popularity of horror movies. But when we suffer trauma, this effort to find a means to make sense of our fears can have unintended side effects."

"Really think all alien abduction cases can be explained this way?"

she pressed.

Evans smiled, enjoying the challenge. "Now I didn't say all cases, but consider this: it was not until our modern technological age that alien abduction stories really took off. We were deep into the Cold War. The space-race was upon us. It's quite convenient that every abduction story seems to describe technology that is very akin to the existing technology of its day. Compare abduction stories from the 60s and 70s to those of today. While these beings supposedly have far superior technology than our own and travel impossible distances to reach Earth, there are simply too many gaping holes in any UFO scenario that tries to claim these are, in fact, beings from another planet. And that's without getting into the theories that claim aliens are inter-dimensional travelers." He couldn't help but roll his eyes.

"At any rate," he continued. "Our brains can often fixate on new information and try to fit things into a particular pattern, especially if we become preoccupied with some new info we perceive as a threat or as exciting. With UFOs, it's known as the 'space-flight effect.'"

"Which is what?"

"In the late fifties, there was this period of about a month after the very first couple of man-made satellites were launched that everyone was obsessed with space. It was finally setting in for people that space was our new frontier for discovery. And in that month that followed those two launches, the reports of UFOs shot up by a factor of seven."

Mitchell nodded, continuing to look about.

"You know," Evans added, "in 1961, the case that started the modern alien abduction era took place not far from here."

"You mean that couple?" Mitchell asked.

"Betty and Barney Hill," he nodded. "Chased by a UFO down the highway."

"What about Roswell? That happened before the Hills case."

"Ah, Roswell. 1947, actually, well before the Hills' case, but Roswell wasn't an abduction case. They merely found the wreckage of a crashed UFO," he smiled. "Allegedly. But you should know better than me, right? You work for the government."

She smiled. "We can't figure out which politicians have engaged in campaign finance fraud, so don't think that anyone has told us where Area 51 is."

"Campaign finance fraud?" Evans scoffed. "That's easy. All of them!"

Mitchell laughed. "Right! But what are you really getting at?"

"All I'm saying is that aliens are just old superstitions reinterpreted to fit our modern scientific age," he shrugged.

She grew serious now and said, "Seems like a convenient theory. It's a mental health problem. Let the therapist fix it."

Evans frowned, taken aback. It was suddenly clear to him that they were far from being on the same page on this still. Before thinking, he spoke. "And your theory isn't any less convenient? There must be someone doing this. That way, the FBI agent can arrest them."

Immediately, Evans regretted his tone. It was too defensive. He wasn't thinking clearly on an empty stomach. Mitchell stared at him, then, slowly, she cracked a smile.

"Well, there's a little fight in you after all," she remarked. "Not used to seeing this side of you, doc." She looked around at the trees. "I'm not finding much out here," she said.

Relieved, Evans let his guard down and pounced on this opportunity. "Come on," he said. "Let's go eat something good. The FBI's buying."

"You know, you're a lot more snarky when you're not my therapist," Mitchell smiled.

"Well, I wasn't hungry then," he shot back as he turned and headed for the car.

She laughed. "Fine, I get the hint. Let me just check around the edge of the road on the other side, and then we'll go."

CHAPTER EIGHT

BLACKNESS. A CHILL BREEZE swept over her body. She could feel the cold hard metal table beneath her. Stephanie gasped with the sudden realization of where she was. A powerful light burst to life over her suddenly and moved down closer to her with a robotic whir. She tried to look about, but was only able to move her eyes. Something prevented her from moving her limbs. Her whole body felt like a dead weight. She knew where she was: she was on the ship, laying nude on one of their horrible examination tables. Fear gripped her as she tried to will her body to move. All she managed to do was to slightly lift her head from the table. She was able to see that nothing held her to the table, but her body tingled all over with the sensation of an invisible force that prevented her from being able to rise and flee.

Summoning all her willpower, she managed to force a single word out that fell from her mouth like a hoarse croak, "Hello?"

Only darkness surrounded the table. She saw nothing beyond what was immediately illuminated by the light overhead. Her heart raced.

She wanted to believe it was just a dream, just a nightmare she could escape if she could only will herself to wake up. But the cold air against her skin, the slight smell of sulfur, the way her throat ached for water told her this was no dream.

"Please," she managed to say, "let me go. Please."

She felt a tear slip out of her eye and travel down towards her ear as she lay there. What could she do? Nothing, the thought invaded her mind. I can't do anything. I never can do anything.

From the darkness, she heard movement. She strained her neck and eyes trying to look down the length of the table, past her feet, and into the darkness where the noise had come from. Slowly, a grey shape emerged from the darkness and stood at the foot of the examination table. It's large head tilted down. It's large black eyes looked at Stephanie. She wanted to scream at it, but she had no strength to do so. The alien simply stood there, staring down at her. She hated it. She hated how it looked, how it stood, how those black eyes seemed to look at nothing and everything at the same time. She hated that she had no control, no power, no protection, that she lay there completely vulnerable and exposed.

Do not be afraid, came the uninvited thought to her mind. She stared at the alien being, feeling enraged by this new invasion of her person. It was in her head now. It was as if she could feel it moving around the rooms of her mind, searching, digging. What was it after?

"Stop," she whimpered.

We are here to help you, came the response in her mind.

"Please," she said, "let me go."

She wanted to scream. She wanted to ask it why they had to take her. Why did she have to be paralyzed, naked, humiliated?

Our ways are different than yours, came the response. We are here to bring help to the human race. You are special. You have been chosen.

This is a great privilege.

It sure as hell didn't seem like a privilege to Stephanie. The words that were being projected into her mind were soothing on the surface, but she couldn't shake the sense of dread within her.

"Everything is okay," said a voice to her right.

She strained her neck and eyes forcing her head to move so she could see who stood there now. The voice had been human, a boy's voice. Finally, her eyes caught a glimpse of who stood just next to the table. It was the boy from the picture, the boy that had gone missing: Tommy Ferguson. He appeared to be naked himself. The look on his face seemed placid as he stood there looking at her.

"Everything will be fine, Stephanie," he said to her. "We're here to help you. We're here to help everyone."

An odd smile took over the boy's lips, but only his lips. His eyes remained fixed on hers, though they seemed vacant. From behind Tommy, a grey hand with long fingers reached out of the darkness and came to rest on his left shoulder. Slowly, another grey alien stepped closer and stood just behind Tommy, now visible in the light.

"Come be with us," Tommy said.

This was too much for her and Stephanie summoned what remained of her strength and willpower. She screamed. As she did so, she felt cold hands from all around reach out and take hold of her body. The light vanished.

STEPHANIE CONVULSED AS SHE fought the hands that held her. Her eyes opened and she saw light again. But now she saw the white walls of her room in St. Jerome. Two nurses, one male and another female, tried to hold her down as her arms and legs flailed about. There was an awful howling sound that horrified Stephanie. Slowly, she realized that she was the one making that unearthly sound. She regained control of her body and gasped for breath.

"Everything's okay, Stephanie," the female nurse said to her. "Everything's okay. It was just a dream. You're safe."

Stephanie looked around, confused. Had it been just a dream? Though she lay on her bed in the hospital gown, she still felt the cold metal of the examination table pressed against her back. Her throat still ached for water. Her body still tingled slightly from whatever invisible force had held her down.

As she breathed hard, trying to regain her composure, a new sensation came to her. She felt a stinging on the back of her neck. The nurses released her now but stood looking at her as she lay on her bed. Slowly, Stephanie reached back and touched her neck. She felt something on her fingers. Pulling her hand back, she saw blood on her fingers. The nurses, seeing this, became alarmed.

"What happened?" the male nurse asked.

They helped her sit up, and the male nurse pulled her hair aside to look at her neck.

"Oh my god," he said. "She's scratched the hell out of her neck. We're going to need to clean that up."

The female nurse stood quickly and bolted out of the room. The male nurse looked at Stephanie with concern.

"Did you scratch your neck?" he asked her.

Stephanie looked down at her hands. She had reached with her left hand just then to touch her neck. The fingers on that hand were stained with blood of course. But she looked at her right hand and noticed that they too were stained with blood. But not on the pads of the fingers like she'd touched her neck with that hand as well. There was blood under her finger nails. She'd done this to herself.

MITCHELL LOOKED AT THE fragile girl before her. Stephanie seemed even more of a girl now than when she'd first seen her. Her hair was a mess and her face pale as she sat on her bed in her hospital gown, her back against the wall behind her. Evans and Mitchell sat in chairs that had been brought into Stephanie's room.

"Stephanie," she said. "It's Agent Mitchell. Do you remember me?"

Stephanie nodded.

"Dr. Evans and I would like to ask you some questions, if that's okay," Mitchell said, softly.

Again, Stephanie nodded.

"Stephanie," Evans spoke up, "did you have a nightmare?"

Stephanie looked off now, saying nothing. They watched her, waiting. At last, she nodded.

"Can you tell us what it was about?" Evans asked.

"I don't want to," Stephanie said softly.

"I know it must be really scary," Evans said, maintaining a soothing tone. "We just want to help you. You can tell us anything."

At this, Stephanie looked at him for a moment. Then she looked to Mitchell. She seemed to be considering whether or not she could trust them. Mitchell waited, doing her best to communicate empathy and safety with open posture and eye contact.

"I was in this ..." Stephanie said at last. "This very dark place. It was their ship."

"Can you recall what it looked like?" Evans asked.

"It was all dark," she said, shaking her head.

"What were you doing in this dark place?"

She looked down before speaking. "I was ... on a table. There was a light above me. I couldn't move. I was naked." Those last words were almost a whisper.

"It's okay," Evans said. "You're safe now. Was there anyone there with you?"

"Not at first," she said.

"Who else was there?"

"One of them stood at the end of the table," Stephanie said. "He talked to me in my head."

Evans nodded, glancing over at Mitchell. "What did he tell you?"

"That I shouldn't be scared. I was special. I had been chosen."

"And how did you feel?"

"Scared," she said, her voice wavering.

"Why is that?"

"I don't know."

"Was there anyone else there?"

Stephanie looked at Evans now. "That boy was there. That boy that went missing."

"Tommy?" Mitchell asked. Quickly she reached into her bag and pulled out the picture she had of Tommy Ferguson and showed it to Stephanie. "You saw this boy?"

Stephanie nodded, "He was naked too. Just standing there. And he was with them. One of the aliens stood there with him."

"Stephanie," Mitchell said, leaning in closer, "the other day, when we showed you this picture of Tommy Ferguson, you said something. Do you remember what you said?"

Stephanie looked at her in bewilderment. She shook her head.

"You said something to us about being taken to join Tommy in three days. Do you remember that?" Mitchell pressed.

Stephanie looked from Mitchell to Evans, clearly confused. Again she shook her head.

"Are you sure?" Mitchell tried again. "I know this is hard, but I need you to think carefully about—"

"NO!" Stephanie screamed suddenly. "Just stop! Leave me alone!"

Stephanie turned on her bed, pressing her right shoulder against the wall so she was turned away from them and facing the window. Tears flowed from her eyes and she fought to control her breathing as her body shook.

"We just want to help, Stephanie," Evans tried to reassure her.

"Well, you're not helping!" she shot back.

Evans looked to Mitchell shaking his head slightly. They were done for now.

"We're going to let you rest," Evans said to her. "Your parents will be here in a bit. If you need anything, we'll be here. Just call the nurse."

Stephanie did not look at him. She stared out the window that showed only the yellow glow of a lamp outside on the hospital grounds. Night had set in hours ago. And with the dark clouds that hung over the area, it was a particularly dark night.

Evans and Mitchell rose to leave. They stepped out of her room and headed down the long hallway. As they did so, the male nurse on duty turned the corner and was immediately followed by the Clarks. They headed towards them. Mitchell wondered if they had been awoken. She and Evans had previously gotten dinner and then headed back to look at more of the old case files. Nothing else proved to be as interesting as the discovery of Pastor Diego's report. Either way, they had still been up. The Clarks, on the other hand, looked positively exhausted. But this probably had more to do with the stress of the past few days. Likely, they too had been up simply because sleep didn't feel like a viable option given the circumstances.

They passed each other in the hallway with only brief eye contact. Tim gave a slight nod. Dorothy looked at Evans and Mitchell with her wide concerned motherly eyes. They continued down the hall, their footsteps echoing against the old brick walls. Overhead, a florescent light buzzed oppressively as Mitchell and Evans walked away. Mitchell felt helpless. What could she do to stop this?

"Do you buy it?" she asked Evans.

"The abduction story?" he said, glancing over at her as they walked. "It's consistent with other such cases."

"Right. But do you believe it when she says she doesn't remember what she said the other day?"

"She's clearly suffered some serious psychological trauma. I'm sure the past few days will forever be hard for her to recall."

Everything seems hard for Stephanie to recall, Mitchell thought. Then a new thought popped into her head. What if they could help Stephanie recall? She grabbed Evans's arm, stopping him before they reached the waiting room entrance. He looked at her, surprised.

"Then, let's help her recall," she said.

"What do you mean?" Evans frowned.

"Hypnosis," Mitchell said softly. "It's a common practice in abduction cases."

She could see hesitation in Evans's eyes. He sighed, looking off. "Hypnosis can be a wonderful thing," he said. "I've used it with certain patients."

"But?" Mitchell prompted.

"Under hypnosis, people have a high level of suggestibility. Especially in a case like this, it may be too easy to introduce more suggestions of alien abductions into Stephanie's mind rather than uncovering the truth."

"If there's any truth to what she said—that in three days she would be taken to join Tommy—then we're going to lose Stephanie in less than 48 hours," Mitchell said softly but firmly, her eyes locked on his.

"We have to try something."

Evans looked at her for a long moment, his eyes moving back and forth as if reading her own eyes, sizing her up. She remained still, waiting.

"You're serious about this?" he whispered.

"I just want to uncover the truth," she said. "And either way: we might find some deep emotional trauma that is behind all of this, or we might just get some clue as to who is doing this. I think it's all we have left. In the days before Tommy went missing, he had similar nightmares, he was a nervous wreck. He couldn't go to school, he couldn't sleep, he couldn't go play with friends. He was in constant fear. He would have sudden outbursts of anger, just like we just witnessed. And then ... one day he was just gone."

Evans sighed again, looking off and thinking all of this over. She waited, knowing there was no sense in pushing but hoping he would understand the urgency. What other options did they have at this point?

"If we do this," Evans looked back to her now, "we have to be careful not to influence her. We can't force her to recall things that didn't happen. That won't help us or her."

Mitchell nodded. Evans looked back down the hallway towards Stephanie's room. By now the Nurse and the Clarks had entered the room. The hall with its buzzing fluorescent lights stood stark and empty.

"And we have to clear this with her parents first," Evans said with a note of finality.

Mitchell looked back down the hallway as if she expected to see something. She thought of talking to the Clarks and trying to explain all of this to them.

"We have our work cut out for us," she said.

"What you're asking," Tim Clark said, his voice heavy, "seems dangerous."

The four of them sat in the waiting area of St. Jerome. Mitchell had presented the idea of hypnosis and then had looked to Evans. He took over explaining how the hypnosis process would work and why it could prove quite helpful. In silence, Tim and Dorothy soaked all of this in. Finally, Evans had finished talking. After a moment, Tim had finally spoken.

"I assure you that Dr. Evans is a highly trained professional," Mitchell said.

Dorothy glanced over at her husband. Tim's jaw remained firm, almost clenched. Dorothy, on the other hand, seemed potentially open to the idea. Could it really be? Tim sighed heavily, looking up at the ceiling.

"Our daughter has been through a lot," he said. "She's in a very fragile state as it is. It just doesn't strike me as a good idea to make her relive whatever has happened to her."

As he spoke, Mitchell heard someone come through the front doors. Glancing over, she saw it was Pastor Diego. He spotted them right away, but waited near the door rather than approaching.

"You're right, Mr. Clark," Evans said. "Stephanie has been through a lot, but I sincerely believe she is strong. It's clear to me that her subconscious mind is battling something traumatic. And while it can be scary to confront trauma head-on, it's the only way forward."

"The only way forward?" Tim said, making no attempt to hide how dubious he felt this notion was.

"She's repressing memories of traumatic events," Evans continued in an even tone. "As long as Stephanie is not able to confront and properly deal with whatever is the true cause of all of this fear and anxiety, she will continue to be tormented."

Tim looked down, saying nothing.

"Mr. Clark, I assure you my only goal is for Stephanie to find healing from all of this," Evans said. He glanced over at Mitchell before continuing. "We just want to help Stephanie."

"So do we," said Tim.

And with that he stood and moved to the door. Dorothy shot an apologetic look to Mitchell and Evans before following him. Reaching Pastor Diego, Tim stopped. They spoke in hushed tones. Tim glanced back at Mitchell and Evans for a second as Dorothy joined them. She, however, said nothing.

"That went well," Evans sighed.

Mitchell, eyes still locked on Diego and Tim, said, "Do parents often refuse hypnotherapy?"

"It's not everyone's cup of tea, that's for sure," Evans shrugged. He looked over at the trio talking by the door. "Especially if they happen to have some religious objection to hypnosis."

"He didn't say so," Mitchell pointed out. "Or maybe that's not the issue. Maybe there's something he doesn't want you digging up during hypnosis."

As she said this, Diego happened to glance in their direction. For a brief second, he locked eyes with Mitchell, then nodded. Was he simply being polite? Was he toying with her? She was having a hard time reading this guy.

"So you think Stephanie's father has something to hide after all?" Evans asked, a bit surprised.

Mitchell sighed. "Just considering all possibilities."

CHAPTER NINE

EVANS YAWNED AS HE stared down at his laptop. He had his computer and his notebook set out on the bed of his motel room. Since getting back to the motel, he'd started typing up notes he'd made that day, going into further detail now as he worked on his computer as more observations and questions occurred to him.

Picking up his notebook, he leafed through it, looking over the notes he had made the last couple of days to make sure he'd caught everything. He'd made note of certain common occurrences for alien abductees. Stephanie seemed to have experienced missing time, which was often reported by people claiming to have seen a UFO or had a close encounter of some variety. Even Pastor Diego's story contained this detail. What had he said? Nearly forty minutes had passed when it had only felt like a couple of minutes? Could it be that all of these people were actually experiencing something quite real?

Evans chuckled. Get a grip, he told himself. You have a bad enough reputation as it is. Don't become one of those shrinks that actually thinks his patients are communing with beings from another world.

No, missing time was actually connected to other psychological disorders. People who suffered seizures might not be able to account for several minutes or an hour, especially people suffering from psychomotor epilepsy. In those cases, seizures manifest in various forms of random behavior that people couldn't always account for and often had no recollection of. The amount of time that lapsed during a seizure seemed missing to them. People who suffered a traumatic event often could not recall such an event or even the time around it. Evans had treated a patient about four years prior who had witnessed a horrible accident that involved his daughter. The shock was too great and he'd repressed the memories surrounding the event. The problem was, he struggled to accept the loss of his daughter. His mind became stuck in a loop of denial, unable to accept the reality of her loss and move on. Evans wondered if Stephanie had witnessed something traumatic that she was repressing. Clearly, her lack of memory of her abductions seemed like repression of memories. But could she really be repressing memories from multiple abductions? It seemed almost too neat, too ... engineered.

That is, if she was being abducted at all, by aliens or persons.

Turning back to his laptop, he pulled up a search engine and typed in "signs of alien abduction." He wondered what other details he might be overlooking as far as common occurrences in relation to alien abduction cases. Of course, the Internet was filled with all kinds of pseudo-information when it came to anything paranormal. But even pseudo-information generally found its inception in some tiny bit of misunderstood reality. He browsed through the results for a moment, clicking a few and then abandoning the pages quickly when it seemed clear to him that they were too kooky. For some people, when it came to anything related to UFOs, confirmation bias was so strong that anything, no matter how remote and unlikely, counted as evidence and any counter evidence, no matter how strong, was automatically disqualified. It bothered him that so much of the folklore surrounding UFOs was so easily explained away with a rudimentary understanding of science. Yet, facts didn't seem to matter to such folks.

At last, he found a rather extensive list of "symptoms" people who claim to have been abducted seemed to experience. First on the list was missing time. Second were marks on the body the person could not account for. Third was the sense of constantly being watched. Stephanie had definitely described all three. Fourth was hearing tapping or humming sounds. He paused and read that one more closely. Apparently many people experiencing UFO or abduction related events reported hearing such sounds around bed time or at night. These were sounds unassociated with their living environment and did not occur on a regular basis. But when they were heard, that meant some kind of event would follow that night, ranging from UFO sightings to abductions.

This went on and included things like waking up in a state of fear or panic for no discernible reason, a sense of being special, a fear or aversion to seeing pictures or drawings of grey aliens with large black eyes, waking with soreness in genitals without any explanation, electronics malfunctioning randomly, and so forth. Evans skimmed through the list, quickly noting that many of these symptoms could easily be accounted for by many other psychological disorders, emotional issues, or far more mundane reasons. Further down the list, one symptom caught his eye. He smiled with amusement. It read: "being afraid of closets or doors." He read through the description for it. Apparently, some people experiencing close encounters or abductions developed a specific fear of bathrooms and closets and hallways, or really of any door that might be left open. Doors needed to be closed at all times for a sense of safety, particularly at night. Such people found it impossible to sleep with a closet or bathroom door open in their room. In fact, apparently this obsession could apply to all doors in a person's living space, leading to a need for double and triple checking that all doors were locked or closed before going to bed. Sounds like OCD tendencies getting mixed into this UFO mess, Evans thought.

But of all the symptoms, missing time remained the intriguing one to him. Here was a rather serious lapse in awareness or consciousness. It could be caused by many things, but it seemed indicative to him of rather deep troubles. This wasn't like other odd symptoms like hearing humming or tapping sounds that could probably be explained by any number of logical means. He was about to reach out to his computer to close the browser when loud knocking made him jump.

He closed his eyes and smiled, feeling incredibly foolish. Opting to simply close the screen on his laptop, he walked over to the door and reached for the lock. Something stopped him. Maybe it was all this reading about paranoia and fear that was getting to him. Logically, he was sure he could safely open the door and simply find out who was standing out there and what they needed. In all likelihood, it was just Nicole.

Agent Mitchell, he corrected himself. She's not your patient anymore.

In spite of the protests from the logical hemisphere of his brain, he peered through the peephole on the door. Sure enough. He saw Mitchell standing there. Without further hesitation, he unlocked his door and opened it. The moment the door opened, Mitchell began to speak.

"Hey. I wanted to apologize if I pressured you earlier on the whole hypnosis thing. I brought a piece offering."

She held up a six pack of beer from the local brewery. But as she did so, her expression changed as she looked at Evans.

"You alright?" she said.

"Yeah," Evans nodded. "You just surprised me. I was working and ..." He waved his hand in the air, unsure of what he was even going to say next.

"Gets under your skin, doesn't it?" she said, softly.

He looked at her, sensing sympathy from her. "Yeah. Maybe a little."

"Then let's take a break," she said, holding up the beers again.

"So this idiot says to me, 'Oh, shit, I thought you were a cop,'" Mitchell said, smiling. "So I held my badge up again and said, 'What the hell do you think the FBI is?' And he looks at me honestly dumbfounded and says, 'Wait, the FBIs are cops too?'"

They both laughed. Mitchell took another swig of her beer. A slow and steady rain fell outside now. The continuous patter against the roof and window droned on as they spoke.

"All of a sudden," she continued the story, "the meth lab in his basement was totally not his."

"The FBIs," Evans grinned, his eyes a little glassy. "I'm going to have to remember that."

They chuckled, looking towards the window. They sat on the floor, their backs to the bed. The room wasn't particularly big. There was only one uncomfortable chair in the corner. And sitting on the bed and drinking had not seemed appropriate, so here they were. Mitchell took another drink, feeling the buzz for sure now.

"You really think Stephanie's father is a suspect?" Evans asked.

She thought for a moment about steering the conversation away from work. But she caved. "I don't know for sure. But I can't dismiss it. And you brought it up first."

"I was mostly just presenting an alternative theory for

consideration," he said.

"But he could be involved," she pressed.

"Sure. I guess. But what about her mother?"

"You've seen her," Mitchell rolled her eyes. "She defers to her husband on just about everything."

"And there's Pastor Diego," Evans pointed out. "To listen to him, you'd think all this alien stuff is downright chthonian."

Mitchell paused, running the last word through her head a couple of times. Was she that drunk that she couldn't understand him? Was he that drunk that he couldn't talk straight anymore? No, he was barely drinking.

"What now?" she said.

He smiled and said, "Chthonian. It's from classical mythology. Has to do with gods and spirits from the underworld. Sorry. When I get tipsy, I become a bit of a wordsmith."

"Oh my god, nerd alert!" Mitchell spat out, laughing. She looked over at the one empty bottle next to him and the one in his hand. "You've had one and a half. I'm way ahead of you."

She threw back the bottle and finished the little that was left in it.

"After my fiancé left me," Evans said softly, "I decided to cut back on drinking."

Mitchell looked over at him, suddenly feeling guilty about this whole situation. "I'm sorry. I didn't know. Is this okay?"

"I'm not an alcoholic," he said, looking at her. "I just thought, preemptively, I'd avoid numbing my pain with alcohol."

She'd never seen him in this light before. He'd had a fiancé. She'd left him. All the time she'd spent in his office talking about herself, she'd known that of course he was a person with his own story, his own history. But she never knew any of it. Now that she was beginning to see just a hint of this history, she could feel her perception of him changing. She could see the pain in his eyes. It was obvious he didn't drink much. The one and a half beers he'd had gave his eyes a softer look, as if the careful clinical detachment he normally had about him was only another layer of clothing. And now, with the aid of some alcohol, that layer had slowly fallen off. He'd had a fiancé. She left him. It had been painful. So painful he had consciously chosen not to numb it with alcohol. There was some kind of fear around that, she felt sure.

Feeling the heaviness that had suddenly taken over the conversation, she said the first thing that came to her mind: "Hm. So what? You numbed it with a dictionary?"

He laughed. "Yeah. And work."

Mitchell smiled, nodding. "I know something about that."

"Is that what this is?" he asked, looking at her. "Your drive to solve this case?"

"It's my drive to solve every case," she said, looking down at the empty bottle in her hand. She began to pick at the label.

"Even before your partner was killed?"

She kept picking at the label.

"Nicole," Evans said, leaning a little closer, "let me ask you—as a friend—what's back there? What's behind this certainty of yours that there's a person doing all of this?"

She sighed as a corner of the label on her beer bottle ripped off. "Remember how Pastor Diego said he looked into the eyes of evil?" she said after a moment.

Evans nodded.

"So did I," Mitchell said, willing herself to look up at him. "Only the difference was, I was looking into my own eyes."

Evans frowned ever so slightly, clearly unsure of what she meant by this, but he remained where he was, waiting for more.

"Before I joined the FBI," Mitchell reluctantly embarked on the story, unsure of how to even tell it, "I was in the Army. I did two tours of duty in Iraq. I was young and eager to follow orders."

She looked back down at the beer bottle in her hands, thinking. How to put into words what was going through her head, what she had experienced, what she had done?

"You remember Abu Ghraib" she heard herself say. Part of her was self-aware enough to know that her guard was down. Maybe it was the alcohol, maybe it was the fact that she'd gotten used to telling this man her secrets and fears, or maybe it was the sudden new vulnerability she felt coming from him. But she'd just opened a wound she wasn't sure she was ready to deal with here. Either way, it was too late now.

"The prison with all the human right's violations?" Evans asked. "You were there?"

"No," she shook her head. "But we were detaining insurgents. These fuckers had trapped us on a desert road where they'd planted IEDs. When they blew up the front Humvee, we had to stop. The insurgents were on the surrounding hills, raining lead on us. We lost three men, four more injured."

Without giving it much thought, she reached down and tugged her dress shirt on the right side of her stomach and untucked it. She pulled the shirt up to just under her bra, revealing a long raised scar that ran down her ribs to her right hip.

Evans looked at the scar with shock.

"Shrapnel from one of the IEDs," she explained. "Just a glancing blow." She lowered her shirt, not bothering to tuck it in. "Anyway, we called in two Blackhawks and took them down. Killed most of them on the spot, but captured four. We took them back in for interrogation. Over the next weeks, we got orders to do whatever it took to get these guys to talk."

At this, Evans looked off. She imagined he was making the

connections now, starting to see why she'd brought up Abu Ghraib. She recalled the men's bodies, naked and bruised. She recalled the awful gasping for air, the sputtering of water from their mouths. Muslim men stripped as she stood there, a woman. This was a precise measure of humiliation and she'd known it. She remembered helping hold one of the men as they poured water over his face as he was leaned back in a chair, a rag stuffed in his mouth. The memories washed over her with the same chill as the cold water they'd used to waterboard those men. She could smell the sweat and piss of the dank dry room. Officially, they had never done any of these things, but that didn't matter. Officially or not, these were the images that greeted her mind at night when she finally closed her eyes.

She looked up at Evans, hardly able to believe she was saying this, "There are no pictures. No evidence. Not like Abu Ghraib. But we humiliated those men. Stripped them naked and made them crawl like dogs. We did ... horrible things."

She stopped, taking in a deep breath as she tried to will tears to remain locked inside her eyes. "I try to tell myself that I was young and stupid and just following orders. But ... I wanted those assholes to suffer. We lost Greg, Eric, and Dante. Three good men. And I wanted those ... I wanted them to pay for it."

In spite of her best efforts, a tear slipped down her cheek. She wiped it away immediately then forced a smile as she glanced at Evans and said, "Bet you wish I would have told you this during one of our sessions."

Evans swallowed, then said simply, "Have you told anyone else?"

"We should have been court-martialed. But we didn't make the news, so we got away with it. And that, right there ... that's the world we live in. The real world. I wish there was more to this life. But I don't think there is. There's just us, people. And we're capable of doing truly awful things."

She made no effort to hide the self-loathing and bitterness in her voice. What was the point of that? At any rate, there was the answer to his question.

"We're also capable of doing some amazing things," he said softly.

Anger boiled inside her as she shook her head and said, "But there's no justice. My partner was a good man. A good husband and father. Hell, he went to church every damn week. We called him Agent Saint Dale. But some suspected home-grown terrorist, just a stupid kid we were chasing, pulls a gun and does Dale in."

She glared at Evans, suddenly angry at him for her vulnerability. "I should have died that day. If there was any justice, if there was anyone watching out for us like Dale always tried to tell me ... I would have died ... not Dale."

She meant it. How many times had she wished it? Seen it playing out in her mind? Had she just been a yard ahead of Dale instead of a yard behind him ... She pictured again the bullet hitting her chest instead of Dale's. That's how it should have been.

Evans reached out to her, taking her hand. She felt the touch of his hand on hers. When was the last time someone had held her hand?

"Hey," he said. "You can't think that way. We all make mistakes."

"I've made more than mistakes," she spat back. But she didn't pull her hand away. Instead, she stared down at their touching hands. Taking in a deep breath, she then added, "All I'm saying is, yeah, there is evil in this world. And it's us."

Another tear slipped out of her left eye, but she made no move to hide it or wipe it away. It was followed by a tear in her right eye. Evans reached out slowly and with his free hand wiped away first one, then the other tear. As he did so, she looked into his eyes. He was close now. She could feel her heart beating faster. In that moment, she felt more naked than she'd ever been in her life. They sat there fully clothed, but she had just exposed the dark cloud that hung over her at all times. Evans didn't move away from her. He wasn't appalled or angry or repulsed. He was touching her! She hadn't expected this.

Maybe it was the alcohol, maybe it was the act of emotionally disrobing before this man, but the room spun around her. She closed her eyes to steady herself, feeling his hand on her cheek, the other hand holding hers. Some part of her mind still capable of a semblance of objectivity in this state recognized what she did next as some sort of mix of instinct and choice.

She leaned in and kissed Evans.

CHAPTER TEN

She drew in a sharp breath. Her heart raced. Her eyes opened, trying to lock on anything familiar. It took her a second to recall where she was. Stephanie sat up in her bed in her room at St. Jerome. Only a dim yellow light from one of the outside lamp posts leaked through the window. Rain drops rolled down the glass, casting indistinct moving shadows on the wall by her bed. Her eyes darted to each corner of the room quickly. She was alone.

She wasn't even sure she'd had a dream. She'd just woken up suddenly as if a nightmare had simply intended to visit her, leaned down by her bed, and whispered in her ear. It had been enough. The familiar but always unwelcome feeling of being watched washed over her. She twisted around in bed, again checking every corner from where she sat. Her whole body ached as if her muscles had been all strained or overexerted somehow. But she had been nowhere.

She placed a hand on the cold cinderblock wall next to her bed. The cold on her hand reminded her of the table. The cold metal table. The image of those eyes—those big solid black eyes like an abyss—flashed into her mind involuntarily. They were coming for her, she was sure of it. They would come for her even here. There was nowhere she could be safe. Slowly, she moved her body around so it pressed against the wall. She gathered her legs up in front of her, wrapping her arms around them. There was no point in laying back down; she might as well wait.

What did they want with her? Why her? Why was she taken so many times? Why couldn't they explain what they were doing? If they were here to help her, to help all of humanity, why couldn't they simply tell her what they needed to do? Why did they have to treat her like some animal, some lab rat? If they could look into her mind and speak to her so directly, why not give her the knowledge she needed to understand what was happening to her?

Unless ... they didn't want her to have that knowledge.

She swallowed, wishing she could run, but she knew the door was locked. She was in a fucking mental hospital. It's not like they were about to believe her if she banged on the door and told them, "aliens are coming to get me." Hell, she wasn't even totally sure she could believe it herself. But here she was. Part of her sincerely wanted to believe she was simply crazy. *Wouldn't it be so much easier if I was just batshit crazy?* She wiped away a tear knowing all too well she wasn't crazy, not at least in the sense in which the hospital staff thought she was crazy.

Or her father. Fuck him! Why couldn't he just believe her? But he was a conventional man trying to preserve a conventional life. She was sure he just desperately wanted everything to get back to normal. She pictured him at his desk at the bank, filling out paperwork with people applying for a small business loan or refinancing their mortgage, the whole time squirming under his skin as he worried about what they must be thinking of him due to his crazy daughter who believes she's being abducted by aliens. She wanted to hate him. But no ... really, she wanted him to hold her. She too wanted everything to go back to normal, but part of her did hate him for not believing her, for abandoning her here.

She sat there for a while, staring at the opposite wall. She lost track of time as thoughts about her father, her mother, her friends who hadn't bothered to come by and see her, tossed and turned in the choppy waters of her mind. She had no real way of knowing how much time was passing. When the slight tapping sounds began, she knew what was happening. Her heart raced, her palms were wet with anticipation. But she clenched her teeth and thought, I'm not going anywhere, assholes. Let's get this over with.

When the bright light burst through her window, she wasn't surprised. But she noted it was red now. It had always been blue before. The red light swung up from the floor and filled the room. As it crept over her body, she could feel the tingling, the coldness, the numbness. She gripped her legs tighter to her chest and closed her eyes and waited.

IN THE WAITING AREA, Eliza, the 55-year-old nurse on duty that night, sat at the desk. The small TV on the corner of the large metal desk played commercials as she waited for a late night movie to resume. She didn't even know what movie it was exactly, but it was something to keep her awake while she looked over some paperwork before she had to do her next round of checking in on patients.

Other than the din from the TV and the drizzle of the rain outside, the place was quiet. She looked down at the charts for one of the patients. But as she did so, the lights flickered. The TV blipped and rolled and then returned to normal. She looked up, unconcerned. The building was quite old. Maybe the storm was getting worse? She looked back down at the chart, but again the lights flickered. This time the

TV emitted a sudden burst of loud static. She looked over at it, startled. She'd never seen it do that before!

She stared at the TV for a second, wondering if it might do it again. It didn't. She looked back down at the papers in her hands. The lights flickered again and this time the TV went to static permanently, the speakers blaring as if it were at maximum volume. The noise hurt her ears. She reached out and hit the power button, but it wouldn't turn off. She pressed it several times as the lights flickered off and on sporadically. Giving up on the power button for the TV, she got up and moved to the side of the desk. Finding the power cord for the old TV, she pulled it from the wall.

Silence. The static rang in her ears still, but the place was quiet again. Only the rain outside and the usual slight hum of the fluorescent lights could be heard. But something about how the TV had just behaved filled her with unease. She wondered what she should do. As the lights flickered again, she made up her mind.

She picked up the phone on the desk and dialed. She waited while it rang several times. The lights dimmed for a second, but didn't go out all the way as before. Finally Will, the custodian of the place, picked up.

"Yes?" he said with a croak that made it clear he wasn't thrilled about being woken up.

"Hey, Will," she said, "It's Eliza. Sorry to call so late, but the power's doing weird things here."

"It's just the storm," he said.

"That's what I thought, then the TV did something strange," she said.

"Did what strange?"

She felt foolish. She shouldn't have called. It was fine. The TV was probably broken. It was old. She was about to open her mouth to apologize for bothering him at all in the middle of the night when the lights went out, and this time, they stayed out!

The phone line was dead. She looked over to the emergency lights that should have kicked on the moment they lost power. But they too emitted no light. Setting the phone down, she began digging noisily in the desk drawers for the flashlight. She knew there was one in there, but it had been ages since she'd used it. Now she couldn't recall which drawer it was in. And who knew if it actually had good batteries in it anymore?

She found it at last in one of the drawers. Clicking it on, she was relieved to find that it worked. She looked down at the desk, thinking she should grab her cell phone out of her purse and call Will back. If the emergency lights were out, it had to mean ...

A scream bounced off the walls of the old building and echoed in the darkness. Eliza stood petrified by the sound of the scream, a chill running down her body. It came from some far recess of the place, and it was the sound of unrestrained terror that sent a sudden shaft of ice into Eliza's heart as she heard it.

She moved to the main hallway and began walking. She wasn't far when the second scream reached her ears. This time, she knew who was screaming. With all the activity lately, with the local police and the FBI there, she knew just where the screams were coming from. She'd heard her scream before.

Eliza ran as fast as her bad left knee would allow her to. As she approached Stephanie's room, she slowed so she could fish the keys out of her pocket. As she did so, her flashlight dimmed and went out. Eliza cursed as she smacked it. A dim beam emitted from it again. She found the keys and unlocked Stephanie's door.

Swinging the door open, she pointed the dim flashlight in. First she trained it on Stephanie's bed, but found it empty. Then she swept it around the back wall. The light fell suddenly on a figure in the back left corner opposite the bed. It was Stephanie. She crouched in the corner, her head down.

"Stephanie?" Eliza said. "Are you okay?"

Slowly, Stephanie looked up at her. She locked eyes with Eliza, but her eyes seemed completely vacant. It was only as Eliza moved the dim flashlight beam up to follow Stephanie's head that she noticed something behind Stephanie. She moved the dim beam up the slender grey body to the large grey head. It looked down at Stephanie.

When Eliza moved her lips to speak, the thing's head jerked up suddenly and its large black eyes locked on her. She felt a sudden rush of uncontrollable panic. Stumbling backwards, she screamed as she fell into the hallway, the flashlight clattering to the floor. It went out and she was plunged into blackness again. But all her focus was on getting away from whatever was inside that room with Stephanie. As Eliza struggled to her feet, her bad left knee biting sharply with pain, she heard the door to Stephanie's room slam shut in the darkness.

EVANS FELT LIGHTHEADED. WAS this really happening? Mitchell pressed her lips against his. He responded instinctively, kissing back. A rush of heat came over him and he reached out his right hand, gently taking hold of her head. He had not kissed a woman in over two years. He had not touched a woman at all, in fact. They parted for a second, looking into each other's eyes. The question between them in that moment was clear. Proceed or not? Throw caution to the wind or call it a night?

They both stood quickly, eyes locked on each other. Mitchell didn't move for the door the moment she stood, as part of Evans had expected. Some part of Evans's mind that was not yet thrown off by his low tolerance for alcohol or the sudden rush of desire observed all of this as it happened from a relatively objective perspective. This was wrong. He knew it was wrong. Two weeks ago, Nicole had been his patient. But another thought occurred to him: there was no denying that she was attractive. And even in all of his professional distance, that simple recognition that an attractive and compellingly confident woman had walked into his office remained from his first impressions of her. Working together in this capacity, the relationship had deepened, evolved, undergone an unexpected metamorphosis within the constraints of the case and the pressure to resolve this quickly. And now, tonight, this new openness unlocked something even deeper.

Mitchell kept her eyes locked on him. Again, he noted she had not moved to the door. She was breathing quickly with the sudden rush of excitement. It was the smallest thing that pushed Evans over the edge. She was breathing through her mouth ever so slightly. She licked her lips to remoisten them, and then for a split second lightly bit her lower lip. That subtle gesture was all he needed. He reached out and pulled her close to him and they kissed again. She reciprocated with surprising force, kissing him hard, her arms wrapped around him tightly, fingernails biting his back. For so long, Evans had forced his mind to remain always analytical, coolly detached from the moment, in hopes of always making an intellectual decision. Now, thoughts rushed through his brain like: she knows what she wants and will likely take the lead here; she hasn't had a relationship in about as long as I have; we're not thinking clearly; if anyone finds out, this could be serious trouble for us both.

But there was no time for that. Nicole was pulling his shirt up. They parted long enough for Evans to pull his dress shirt off like a t-shirt. With the top button undone, it wasn't too hard. Next, his white undershirt went off, tossed aside by Mitchell. She pulled him close and kissed him again. Her shirt was already partially untucked from when she'd shown him her scar. He pulled it out the rest of the way, but pulling it over her head like she had done with his wasn't exactly an option with her fitted women's dress shirt. Before he could make a move, she was already unbuttoning her shirt, still kissing him in the process.

Mitchell's cell phone rang.

They froze, faces inches apart. The phone rang again. Both Evans and Mitchell glanced at the alarm clock sitting on the end table. It displayed 3:09 AM. Something had happened!

"I should get that," she said, softly.

"Yeah," Evans agreed.

Mitchell backed away from him and grabbed her purse that sat on the floor next to the door. She reached down and grabbed her phone, answering. She stood, phone pressed to her ear.

"This is Agent Mitchell," she said into the phone, her voice all business now.

As she listened, Evans waited. She stood there, shirt hanging open, eyes focused on some invisible point far off as she took in what was being said. Conflicting thoughts within Evans's mind battled for his attention. He knew this was probably the best thing that could have happened. He knew there must be something incredibly important going on for Mitchell to get a call at 3:00 AM—there was that time again; 3:00 AM. And yet, he couldn't keep from looking at Mitchell and thinking of what could have happened—what would have happened. A very real part of him that he'd silenced for a long time now screamed with fury and desire. If only her phone had been silenced. If only the call had come just a little later. If only. But he knew, this was for the best. It just didn't feel like it right then.

Mitchell's eyes grew wide as she listened. Suddenly, she snapped her fingers to get Evans's attention, pointing to his shirt and then to the door. They had to go.

"I'll go get Dr. Evans and we'll be right there," she said into her phone. Then hanging up, she locked eyes with Evans, who was in the process of putting his undershirt back on. For a moment, her mouth opened as if she were about to say something, but she sighed instead. Looking down, she began to button her own shirt as she said, "Can you drive?"

MITCHELL BLINKED, TRYING TO clear her head. Evans sat behind the wheel, driving her car to St. Jerome's. Her hands shook slightly. She knew it wasn't the alcohol. Her entire body still buzzed from the rush of pent-up desires. She knew it wasn't all about Evans. But she also knew she had denied herself sexual release for quite a long time. She realized now how stupid she had been. She should not have gone over there with the beers. They should have gotten some sleep. Now they hadn't slept at all that night, and their professional relationship had taken a sudden turn.

Anger at herself boiled inside her. Mitchell had always been cautious. She knew the kind of world she lived in. It was still a man's world. But in the army and in the FBI, she felt the glares from other women. She knew how some women talked to her about other women and could only imagine they talked about her the same way behind her back. An attractive woman rising through ranks, getting the fast track into the FBI ... she must be doing someone some favors, right? She had never done any such thing. She had never gotten involved with anyone she worked with. But tonight, she nearly blew that record.

Or had she blown that record already? They hadn't slept together, but they were well on their way there when the phone rang. She couldn't escape the notion that no matter how she looked at what had just happened, a line had been crossed. Now, it could be added to her long list of reasons why she hated herself.

"What exactly happened?" Evans asked, suddenly bringing her back out of the tangled web of thoughts.

"Stephanie had some kind of freak out," she answered. "Not sure of the details, but the nurse on duty called the cops."

"Because a patient freaked out?" he glanced over at her in confusion.

"They said she saw something," Mitchell said.

"Like what?"

"I don't know," she shook her head.

They grew silent as Evans drove. Outside, the rain had slowed to just a slight drizzle. Periodically, the wipers swung up across the windshield to clear it. For a few long minutes, the sound of the engine and tires on the wet road interrupted every now and again by the slight squeak of the wipers was all Mitchell heard. She could feel the tension that now loomed between them. The drive was too long. They would have to talk, wouldn't they? But she didn't even know where to start. But in the end, she didn't have to start it.

"Nicole," Evans said, his voice low. "I'm really sorry."

"About what?" she said automatically, not sure how to go from here.

Evans spoke with his eyes forward, concentrated on the driving, while he slowly worked the words out of his lips, "What happened back there. What was about to happen. It was unprofessional."

Mitchell glanced at him. She knew what he was saying was true, but she felt angry at him for saying it that way. Was he implying she was unprofessional? Or was he the unprofessional one?

"You're not my therapist anymore," she said before she even realized it.

"It's still," he sighed, "not right."

She knew this. Knew it full well. And yet, hearing him say it like that infuriated her. She felt lectured, talked down to. She scoffed and looked out her window.

"I'm sorry," Evans continued. "Look, I'm honestly attracted to you and I think it's starting to cloud my judgment. And I think you need more help, but now it would be highly inappropriate ..."

"I need help, huh?" she spat out as she spun to face him. "Do you ever turn your therapist voodoo on yourself? I'm pretty sure you need help too. So fuck you!"

He looked over at her. She could see the hurt in his eyes. "Well," he said slowly, "You were about to, but then your damn phone rang."

He returned his attention to the road. Mitchell stared at him in disbelief. A slight laugh escaped her lips. She smiled in spite of herself. She most definitely had not expected that response! As a grin cracked over Evans's face, she was not able to contain herself and laughed outright. Evans laughed too, the tension defusing.

Everything went dark!

The car's engine died. All the lights on the dash were out. The headlights were out. Their laughter stopped abruptly.

"What did you do?" Mitchell asked.

"I didn't do anything," he shot back.

The car coasted to a stop on the dark country road. They were well outside of any town and out there on a rainy night, there was little light to offer them much help in seeing what was happening. Mitchell hoped that any car that might be coming down the road behind them might see them in time to stop or avoid them, but it was very late and they had not seen another car in quite a while, so they were likely fine.

She pulled out her cell phone. Hitting the home button to bring it to life, she saw that it was now 3:16 AM. But before she could unlock the phone, the screen went blank. She tried the home key again, then the power button.

"My damn phone just died," she said.

A bright light exploded out in front of them, blinding them. Mitchell shielded her eyes. It was definitely not a car. It was too bright, and seemed to be coming from a rather high source.

"What the hell is that?" Evans said, his own arms raised to block the light.

Instincts took over. Feeling cornered but also feeling sure this light was no accident, Mitchell pulled her gun from its holster in one quick move and opened her door. "Stay here," she barked to Evans.

She stepped out into the blinding light. The steady drizzle filled the air. She raised the gun towards the light with her right hand. With her left, she shielded her eyes. Squinting, she stepped forward.

"I'm a Federal agent and I'm armed!" she shouted. "Turn out that light right now!"

No response came. In fact, there was no sound at all other than the drizzle and a slight breeze that blew through the trees. Then, a slow hum, almost a vibration in the ground and air, began to grow. Mitchell took a few more steps out. Could this really be happening? Her mind raced ahead of her. Could this be whoever was behind Stephanie's abductions?

Another thought pried its way into her mind: could this UFO business be real after all? She pushed the thought from her mind, dismissing it as ludicrous. Still, here she stood on a road with a car that had completely died, no working electronics, and a bright light before her.

The hum grew louder and now the light began to move. It elevated slowly until it was nearly directly above her. She stopped where she was and pointed the gun up. Suddenly, an unexplained panic struck her. What was she doing there? There was nowhere to hide!

Her entire body felt a rush of coldness wash over it as complete silence enveloped her. She suddenly felt quite dizzy.

EVANS WATCHED FROM INSIDE the car as Mitchell stepped out towards the light. *Just what the hell is happening? This can't be real*, he thought. But awareness of UFO cases worked against him. His mind instantly filled with facts: all electronics had stopped working; the light appeared suddenly, was incredibly bright and made no sound; they were driving through an area known for recent abductions and sightings.

He heard the low humming begin. Then the light moved higher until it was above Mitchell. She had her gun pointed straight up. *What is she doing?* Evans moved to open his door as the hum grew so loud it became all he could hear. It vibrated through the car, through his very bones. He threw open the car door and got out.

"Nicole!" he yelled.

Blackness enveloped him. The hum ceased. He couldn't see anything. All he heard was a slight breeze and the continuous whisper of the falling drizzle. It slowly soaked him as he stood there trying to gain his bearings.

"Nicole?" he called out.

Nothing.

Suddenly, light. But this time, it was the headlights of Mitchell's car that began to work again. The car made a dinging sound now as he'd left the keys in the ignition and the door open. He blinked in yet another change of brightness for his eyes to adjust to.

Looking out in front of the car, all he found was empty road. Then his eyes landed on the gun laying on the road where Mitchell had stood.

"Nicole!" he screamed into the night.

He rushed forward, looking around, then up.

She was gone.

CHAPTER ELEVEN

Diego pulled open the door to the waiting area at St. Jerome. He walked in, looking around for any staff. But he found no one at the front desk. Knowing where Stephanie's room was, he headed down the hall. He'd gotten a frantic call from Dorothy, and he'd been awake anyway. It was during his now normal waking hour—his prayer vigil. Something had happened with Stephanie.

He headed down the long white hallway. His footsteps echoed off the walls. Somehow, the place felt even more empty at this hour of night. It reminded him of his visit to an old hospital in Brazil in the middle of the night. His sister had lain in one of the beds, her body hooked up to life support machines that were likely older than she was. It was the last time he'd seen her alive. She never woke up. Poorly kept highways in Brazil were their own form of random cruelty, claiming lives at will. The small car she and two friends had been traveling in had become a twisted metal trap. None of them walked away from the head-on collision with a large truck whose tire had blown, causing the driver to lose control on a particularly bumpy section of road. Just like that, his sister had been taken. So much had changed for him since then.

From a door up ahead on the right side, Chief of Police Wilson stepped out into the hall. He was followed by a female nurse. Diego knew which room they had just come from. As he approached, he could just catch the words as Wilson and the nurse talked.

"You're sure you saw someone?" he asked the nurse.

She looked at him for a moment, then looked away.

"You're not sure?" Wilson pressed.

"It," she fought to make the words come out, "wasn't a person."

Wilson's eyebrows shot up. Now Diego was close and he slowed down, not quite sure if he should interrupt or keep his distance.

"You're not going to tell me you saw ..." Wilson growled in a low voice then trailed off.

"It was in the room with her," the nurse said softly. "It's exactly what I told the other officers."

Diego took this in. Of course, St. Jerome was well outside of North Woodstock. Wilson and his officers would not have been the ones dispatched. But given his connection to this case and the manner in which local police departments collaborated, he was likely notified immediately.

Wilson shook his head then looked up at Diego with a frown.

"The FBI agent and the shrink," Diego lost no time in asking, "are they here?"

"I called Agent Mitchell," Wilson said. "Should be here any minute. Why?"

"No reason," Diego lied. But he could think of no way around it.

"Pastor, I don't know what's going on around here," Wilson sighed, "but I sure as hell am tired of everyone losing their marbles."

Diego saw Wilson's eyes dart over to the nurse. He doesn't believe, Diego noted. He tried to think of what he could say, of what comforting words he might offer in this moment. But Wilson's radio chirped suddenly.

"Chief Wilson, come in," said a woman over the radio.

He grabbed his radio from his uniform belt. "Go for Wilson," he said into it.

"I've got an urgent call from a Dr. Alan Evans," said the dispatcher.

"Jesus!" Wilson rolled his eyes. He glanced at Diego. "Sorry, pastor." He spoke into his radio again as he walked down the hall, "What is it now?"

The radio was too tinny and the sound echoed off the bare walls and was garbled. Diego couldn't make out what was going on. But judging from how Wilson picked up his pace, it wasn't good.

Diego turned to the door and looked in. He found Dorothy and Tim sitting with Stephanie. She was wrapped in a blanket, head hanging down. He stepped closer to the door, but the nurse stuck out her hand, stopping him.

"I'm sorry, who are you?" she asked.

"No, I'm sorry," he said, realizing that of course she didn't know him. "I am Pastor Diego, a friend of the family."

"He's with us," he heard Dorothy say from inside the room.

The nurse glanced over at her and then back to Diego. She nodded and headed down the hallway herself. Diego turned and entered the room. For a moment, a strangely familiar feeling washed over him. It was as if the room had grown just a bit dimmer the moment he stepped in. He looked down at the shaken trio that sat on the bed and his heart broke for them.

THE MAN SLOUCHED BY his car as he filled the tank. The gas station was quiet at this hour, the air hung thick with humidity. The mist of the drizzle that had now become an endlessly moving and swirling fog could be seen in the beams of the overhead lights. He finished filling the tank to his aging Outback and hung the handle up. That's when he noticed her.

She stood just within reach of the lights of the gas station. Immediately, something felt quite off about the scene. He stepped forward, forgetting to retrieve his receipt.

"Are you okay?" he said tentatively.

The woman said nothing. But she looked at him with vacant eyes. She had blond hair that was soaked and stuck to her face and shoulders. Slowly, she stepped closer. As she approached, the man noticed that her dress pants and dress shirt were on inside out. She was barefoot and wore no coat.

"Miss?" the man tried again as she approached him.

She stopped. They were mere feet apart now. The man looked her up and down with concern, wondering what had happened to her. He reached into his pocket to retrieve his phone. But with that movement, the woman sprung at him!

She grabbed his throat and threw him to the ground, knocking the air out of his lungs. The man struggled beneath her, coughing and trying to breathe. He fought hard, finally pulling her hands away from his throat.

"You crazy!" he managed between gasps.

Something changed in the woman's eyes. They focused on him, but now they were no longer vacant. The woman's expression changed to confusion, then fear. She scrambled off of him and collapsed on the wet ground, her back against one of the pumps.

Rubbing his neck, the man pushed himself back against his car, not yet daring to get up. He watched as the woman brought her knees up to her chest, wrapped her arms around them and shook with sobs.

Quickly, he retrieved his phone from his pocket and dialed 911. As he did so, he heard the approaching frantic footsteps of the gas station attendant who was on duty. The woman remained where she was, weeping.

THE RED AND BLUE lights strobed relentlessly. They cast their intermittent light off into the surrounding woods. Evans stared out the windshield of Mitchell's car, which he'd pulled off to the side of the road now. Chief Wilson stood outside his window; the rain had relented, but a mist hung in the air.

"And she just," Wilson lifted a hand, palm up, "vanished?"

"I know how this sounds," Evans said, unable to look at Wilson.

"Has this whole town lost its mind?" Wilson muttered.

Evans looked up at him now, "I'm telling you the truth."

"You said she left her gun behind."

Evans nodded and indicated the gun that now sat in the passenger seat.

"She left it there?" Wilson inquired.

"No," Evans admitted. "She dropped it on the road."

Wilson bent down and looked at the gun then gave Evans a rather dubious look. He sighed, then said, "I'm going to take that gun in and have it checked. For your sake, I hope it hasn't been fired recently."

Evans looked over at him in shock. "You think I did something to her?"

"What I think doesn't matter, Dr. Evans," Wilson said. "But you gotta understand where I'm coming from. I've got a missing FBI agent, her gun has been left behind, and I got your ... story ... that frankly sounds a little absurd. How much have you had to drink tonight?"

Evans froze, still looking at Wilson. His story was about to completely unravel. There was no point in lying now, yet he desperately needed Wilson to believe him. Someone had taken Mitchell—she must have been right after all. There was someone behind this. Someone was doing all of this. Faced with the empty road after the light vanished, the only options left for Evans were to believe someone had taken Mitchell, or something had taken her. Neither now seemed remotely believable as he had tried to explain it to Wilson. He was stuck.

"Dr. Evans?" Wilson prompted him sternly.

"I've," he said, "had ... two beers."

Wilson nodded, his lips pressed firmly together. "I'm going to need you to come with me," he said.

Evans looked up at him. Shit!

"Chief," Officer O'Conner yelled from one of the two police cars parked there. "I just got a call on the radio. They found Agent Mitchell."

Wilson looked back at her. Evans's heart leapt in his chest. They found her! Was she all right?

"Where?" Wilson barked.

"Is she okay?" Evans called out.

"She turned up in Campton," O'Conner said. "She seems fine, but shaken up."

"Campton?" Wilson called back in disbelief.

"Where is that?" Evans asked, but was ignored.

"Should I go get her?" O'Conner asked.

"Yes!" Wilson waved her off. Then turning to Evans he said, "You're coming with me to the station."

"What about Mitchell's car?" Evans asked.

"One of the officers can pick it up."

Evans knew he had no wiggle room at this point. As he got out of the car, Wilson circled around the car and opened the passenger door. He pulled out a plastic bag and with it picked up the gun. Sealing the bag shut he said, "Let's get going, Dr. Evans."

DIEGO WALKED OUT OF St. Jerome. He needed to get home and get some sleep. The Clarks would stay there until morning even though there was little they could do for Stephanie. Diego hoped he could stay awake for the drive home. He would plan on sleeping in late. He had some phone calls to make and he needed to pay a couple of bills, but all of that could wait for the afternoon. He still hadn't gotten started on his sermon for this coming Sunday, but it was early enough in the week he felt he could make up for it at a later time.

Fog hung thick in the air and as he walked away from the old building, it enveloped him in a cloud and the scenery around him became barely visible. Glancing back at the building, Diego noted how menacing and unwelcoming it felt just then. He turned and continued to the parking lot, pulling out his keys. Reaching his truck, he put the key in the door to unlock it, but he stopped suddenly. He was wide awake now. All it took to bring this sudden rush of awareness was the slightest whiff of something. It was a burnt and pungent smell: sulfur.

The hairs on his arms and the back of his neck stood. He knew it stood there behind him before he even turned. But slowly he turned anyway to face it. This one was tall, lanky, dark grey, with large black eyes and slits for nostrils on a noseless face. It cocked its head slowly to one side, seeming to regard Diego with contempt.

Fear washed over Diego. It was an involuntary reaction. The thing just stood there looking at him. Diego could feel the hatred and fear flowing out from this being, and that made him smile.

MITCHELL SAT IN THE same room where she and Evans had searched through the old case files. She now wore spare clothes Officer O'Conner had lent her. She hadn't had a chance to make it back to the motel yet to change. These clothes were just a bit loose. O'Conner was taller. Her own clothing she'd been found in had been soaked, and inside out.

Her body ached, her muscles sore. She still felt cold in spite of the dry clothes and the warm room. Her hair was damp and matted, and she longed for a hot shower. But at the moment, there were questions to answer.

"You said you saw a bright light. What happened then?" Chief Wilson asked. He sat across from her.

Mitchell stared out at the steam emitting from the cup of coffee O'Conner had brought in for her. "I don't know."

"You attacked a man at a gas station. You remember that?"

Disjointed bits of a memory that felt more like a fading dream flashed in her mind. "Yes," she said. Then, "No. Not exactly. I remember seeing his face. He was so scared."

"According to Dr. Evans," Wilson said, "you vanished around 3:15 AM."

"3:16," she said softly. "I looked at my phone just before it died."

"Okay," Wilson nodded, "3:16. You turned up at a gas station in Campton at 3:33 AM. That's ... seventeen minutes. Yet somehow you travelled over 18 miles in that time on windy mountain roads. You'd have to be traveling mighty fast. And I happen to know there were two speed traps set up between where you were taken and Campton. They didn't see any crazy drivers, not that anyone could make that trip that quickly anyway."

"I need to talk to Alan," she said.

"You can see Dr. Evans in a few. First, I need you to answer some questions." Wilson said in a soft yet definitive tone.

Mitchell looked into his eyes and summoned all her will power. "No. I need you to run a tox screen on my blood. Whoever took me must have drugged me."

"Agent Mitchell," Wilson shook his head, "Dr. Evans already admitted that the two of you were drinking. Now, I'm happy to run a tox screen. But if anything does turn up, how do you think this is going to look for Dr. Evans?"

She stared at him in shock now. She couldn't believe what she was hearing. And yet, she could understand how this looked. "You think he drugged me?" she said softly.

"Frankly, I don't know what to think," he said with a sigh. "All I know is that I have a lone FBI agent interfering with an investigation while getting drunk with her psychiatric consultant." He leaned in closer now. "I looked into you, Agent Mitchell. I don't think the Bureau is going to be too pleased."

Mitchell looked at Wilson. She could see his condescension in his body language and eyes. In that moment, she hated him. He now stood squarely in her way. She needed to know what had happened to her, and it most definitely had not been Evans who had done any of this to her.

"I need to talk to Alan," she said slowly but firmly.

Wilson sat back, letting out another sigh. He looked at her for a moment, then tapped his fingers on the table. "Okay," he said at last.

With that he got up and left the room. Mitchell stared at the coffee. Her hands still shook slightly and she figured coffee was actually a terrible idea right now. She would rather have water. She waited for several minutes before at last, the door opened again and Evans walked in.

When he looked at her, she found that she involuntarily got to her feet. He crossed the room and took her into his arms, holding her tight.

"Are you okay?" he asked her.

They parted and she looked into his eyes wanting to convey quickly how committed she was to the words that next came out of her mouth.

"I need you to hypnotize me," she said calmly.

Evans's eyes grew wide. "What?"

"I can't remember anything," she said.

"You're in shock."

"I need you to do this for me," she insisted.

He looked at her, his hands still gently holding her arms.

"Whoever did this just fucked up," Mitchell said in a whisper. "They kidnapped a federal agent. I need to remember what happened. We can stop this!"

Evans looked off, shaking his head.

"It's our only shot, Alan," she said. "Please. Help me!"

CHAPTER TWELVE

Officer O'Conner yawned as she stood next to the police station's camcorder. It sat atop a flimsy tripod. Evans had requested it. Wilson, clearly displeased with the whole situation, had shrugged it off and informed them that come morning, they would need to be out of his station. Mitchell wondered at his seeming lack of objections over what was about to happen. But maybe he was simply too tired to care anymore.

Evans stood by the door and drank a glass of water. A half full glass of water sat before Mitchell on the table next to the coffee she'd never touched. Evans sat down across from her, setting the empty glass on the table. He glanced over at O'Conner.

"Camera good to go?" he asked.

"Yeah," she said.

"Okay then. Roll it," he said.

O'Conner pressed the record button and a tiny red light lit up just above the lens, which was pointed at Mitchell.

Turning back to Mitchell, Evans said, "Okay, Nicole. I need you to close your eyes. Relax your body. Breathe deeply."

She followed his instructions, closing her eyes. She rested her hands in her lap and tried to relax her shoulders. Her breathing slowed as she consciously took control of it.

"Focus on my voice," Evans continued. "I'm going to count back from ten. When I reach zero, you'll be back on the road where we saw the bright light."

She nodded ever so slightly.

In a steady, soft voice, Evans counted down, "Ten. Nine. Eight. Seven. Six. Five."

She felt his voice grow distant. Her body felt heavy, as if it was pulled down by an increase in gravity.

"Four. Three. Two," said Evans's distant voice. "One. Zero."

She felt at first the drizzle, then the gun in her hand. She opened her eyes and what she saw before her was the light. She was out on the road again facing that floating bright light. Her heart began to beat faster now, and with it her breathing became quicker.

"What do you see?" She heard Evans's distant voice ask her.

"The light," she said softly. "Just the light."

"What is the light doing?" Evans asked.

The light moved over her as it had before. "It's moving over me," she said, the whole time watching it.

It stopped above her. She had her gun raised, pointed at it. Again, she felt the panic wash over her. Why was she out there? A rush of coldness washed over her and she grew dizzy. Suddenly all of the air in her lungs was forcibly extracted. She gasped, though she wasn't sure if she gasped only in her memory or if she gasped now as well.

"What is it, Nicole?" Evans said.

She felt her body moving, but she wasn't moving it. Her back was arched as she tried to fight for control, but nothing she did allowed her to will her arms and legs to move. The light increased in intensity, and her whole body tingled as if immersed in a pool of cold bubbling water. Then suddenly, blackness. Silence.

"I can't move," she managed to say. "The light's gone."

"Can you see anything?" asked Evans.

A new light suddenly shone above her. She squinted, trying to get her eyes to focus. Where was she? Slowly, her eyes adjusted and she could see the source of the light was an oblong instrument at the end of an arm that appeared to hang from the ceiling, but she could see no ceiling. Beyond the light there was only blackness. She tried to move, but found that she had no control of her limbs. They were like dead weights her brain had no ability to communicate with anymore.

Slowly, feeling returned to her skin and she became aware of how cold she was. Next, she became aware of how naked she was. She could feel the hard flat surface of the metallic table beneath her. Her heart raced now. What had been done to her? She was no longer sure she wanted to remember what had happened to her, but she fought for composure. If she could remember, maybe she could stop this from happening to anyone else.

But the fear threatened to overwhelm her. A pungent odor reached her nostrils. She tried to kick her legs, and her left foot moved slightly. She craned her head up with all the force she could manage and looked down the length of her body. She saw bizarre instruments and devices around the table. She tried to move her foot again.

Out of the darkness, a slender grey hand shot out and took hold of her left ankle. She screamed. Her body spasmed as a vibration travelled throughout it. It was as if she had been shocked. But it was only the strong vibration of a shock with none of the pain. She lay still now, looking straight up, aware of the cold hand that still touched her ankle.

"What's happening?" She heard Evans's distant voice again.

"I'm on a table," she managed to say. "Like a medical exam. I can't move. I'm naked. And it's so cold. I can smell them. One of them touched me."

"How many are there?" Evans asked.

She forced herself to look around. She realized now that others had crept out of the darkness and stood over her, looking down at her with their black eyes. Their tiny mouths twitched slightly, but they made no sound.

"Yes. Four of them," she said. "Standing around me. Just looking at me."

One of the beings looked at her and she could feel a pressure inside her head as it did so. Suddenly, thoughts that were not her own entered her mind.

Don't be afraid, Nicole. We have come to help you.

She fought to push the voice out of her head, but it repeated itself. A rush of anger caused her to shake slightly where she lay. She couldn't decide which was the worse violation: being forced to lay naked on this metal table like some lab rat to be poked and gawked at, or having her mind invaded. Even the privacy and solitude of her own mind was now being violated, and she hated them for it.

"Are they talking?" Evans said.

"No. They don't talk," she heard herself answer. "Not with their mouths. It's like, they talk to my mind. Telepathy."

"What are they telling you?"

"Not to be afraid. They're here to help us," she said.

She felt tears slip down her cheeks and wondered if this was the memory or the present she felt.

"What's wrong?"

"I don't believe them!"

"Why not?" Evans persisted.

"I don't know. I just don't!"

One of the beings turned to another and nodded its head. That one appeared to punch commands into some sort of command panel attached to a large arm on the table. Another of the beings on the opposite side of the table reached out its hand and touched her stomach just below the belly button. She tried to recoil, but the thing pressed down hard.

Mitchell again tried to force her body to move.

"Nicole, listen to me," came Evans's voice. "This isn't real. Look at them. Look past them."

But she didn't want to look. She just wanted them to stop touching her. A large machine arm swung out over her with an electric whir. A small beam of light emitted from it. It split into a web of light that traveled up and down her body, as if scanning for something. The devices around her emitted sounds and beeps. She wanted to shove it all to the ground, to break out of there. But she felt completely helpless, and she felt terrified by the beings.

"No. No," she whispered. "I can't look at them."

She just wanted it all to end. One of the beings took hold of her head and forced her mouth open. The scanning arm hung over her mouth and emitted light into it.

"It's okay, Nicole," Evans voice came to her. "You said it yourself. They're not real. So unmask them. Look at them for what they really are."

"I'm too scared," she heard herself say in a hoarse whisper, hardly able to get the words out.

"You can do this, Nicole," he said.

She forced her eyes open and she stared up at the being that held her head. She stared into the black chasm that were those oversized shark eyes: eyes devoid of life, eyes that saw no light, but rather sucked all light from her world. She gasped as unrestrained terror washed over her.

MITCHELL CRANED HER HEAD back as she sat at the table in the interrogation room. Evans worried she might hurt herself. Her whole body shook. Tears welled up in her up-turned eyes and ran down her face towards her ears. Her hair, still damp, was a wild tangle. She no longer looked like the emotionally wounded but attractive woman he'd nearly made love to only a couple of hours ago.

He felt the battling forces within him struggling for dominance. He wanted to simply pull her out of her current state and relieve her of her torment. But he also knew that she would be dissatisfied if she couldn't come back from this with valuable information that could prevent Stephanie from disappearing like Tommy.

"Do you see them?" he asked her.

"Yes," she said with difficulty.

She twitched and jerked in her chair and the lights in the room blinked. Evans looked up at the lights then over to O'Conner. She shrugged. It wasn't storming outside anymore. Mitchell still shook in her chair.

"What do you see, Nicole?" he asked.

Her body stopped shaking, but the lights in the room flickered again. She slowly lowered her head until she looked directly at him. Her eyes were focused and yet somehow hollow. For a second, Evans thought she'd come out of her hypnotic state, but she didn't move.

He was about to speak when she said in a low voice, "*Derelinquas nos esse. Non venimus ad te.*"

"What did you say?" he frowned.

"*Derelinquas nos esse. Non venimus ad te,*" she said again, her voice a little louder, but unnaturally low.

"Nicole," Evans said more firmly, though bewildered by this sudden turn. "Focus. Hear my voice."

The room was plunged into darkness. Mitchell screamed now in an unnatural voice, "*Derelinquas nos esse! Non venimus ad te!*"

"Nicole!" he shouted. "I'm bringing you back. I'm going to count back from ten and you're going to wake up. Ten."

"*Derelinquas nos esse! Non venimus ad te!*"

"Nine. Eight. Seven."

"*Derelinquas nos esse! Non venimus ad te!*" she shouted again, her voice becoming higher now.

"Six. Five. Four."

The lights in the room came back on. Evans forced himself to stay focused on Mitchell.

"Three. Two."

Mitchell craned her neck back again, her mouth opening wide. She released a wail that made Evans's heart nearly stop.

"One. Zero."

Silence.

Mitchell slumped in her chair. She breathed hard, exhausted by the ordeal. Perspiration beaded up on her forehead. Slowly, she looked up at Evans, her eyes now wide with fear.

"Nicole?" he said. "Are you okay?"

Slowly, she nodded.

"What were you yelling?" he asked.

She frowned slightly, her mouth dropping open. Her eyes searched his. She looked utterly bewildered by his question.

"I was yelling?" she said at last.

DIEGO STEPPED BACK INTO St. Jerome. How long had he stood out in the parking lot? How much time had he lost? His heart still raced. He felt lightheaded. He approached a male nurse that now sat at the desk. The man was young, probably only in his late twenties. He had wavy dark hair and even in uniform it was evident he was in good shape.

Diego considered how to approach this. But it seemed to him there was little point in being anything other than direct. His body felt heavy and his eyes longed to close. But all the same, his mind was wide awake and nervously buzzing with questions. He could feel his hands shake slightly, and still his knees felt slightly weak. The encounter had taken a lot out of him.

"I need to see Stephanie Clark," he said.

The nurse looked up at him and said, "You a family member?"

"No. Her pastor," he said, knowing full well what this would mean but knowing also that lying here was out of the question as later there would be too many other repercussions to be dealt with.

"I'm sorry," the nurse shook his head. "I have express orders from the police and our head doctor not to let anyone in to see her. Only her parents, and even they were just ushered out of here and told to go home and get some sleep."

"It's an emergency," Diego tried.

"What kind of emergency?" the nurse asked.

Diego looked around, feeling helpless. There was nothing he could say, no way he could spin this and not sound crazy. He had to see Stephanie, that much was clear to him. But how much time did he have? What could he possibly say to this man that would allow him access to Stephanie? The nurse waited with eyebrows raised as if to say, "well buddy, get on with it."

"I really need to see Stephanie," Diego muttered, deflated.

"I don't know what to tell you buddy," the nurse shrugged. "I have my orders. Trust me, she's safe and sound. I just checked on her myself. She's had one hell of a night already, from what I was told. And now she's sleeping it off thanks to what the doc gave her. I think your best bet is to chat with her parents tomorrow once they've had some sleep."

Diego nodded, conceding defeat here. His mind raced ahead of him, considering what the nurse had just said. Talk to Stephanie's parents. He had little option at this point, but he already knew that his chances of explaining himself to them were slim.

"Thank you for your time," Diego said softly as he backed away from the reception desk and headed for the doors.

EVANS STARED DOWN AT his laptop screen. He'd set it out on the table in the interrogation room. A cable ran from the video camera to the computer. To his left, Mitchell sat with a cup of hot chocolate O'Conner had brought to her. O'Conner now sat to Evans's right.

Blinking the fatigue away, Evans scrolled through the video file he'd just copied from the small camcorder's internal hard drive. He tried to suppress a yawn, but it fought its way out anyway. At last, he reached the area where he could see the lights flicker and go out. He scrubbed back in the video and hit play.

"Here," he said to the two women.

On the computer screen appeared the image of Mitchell sitting across from Evans. The view came from just over Evans's right shoulder. Mitchell was under hypnosis; she moved her head back and forth in apparent agitation.

"Look at them for what they really are," came Evans's voice through the tiny laptop speakers.

"I'm too scared," Mitchell responded in the video.

"Wow, I look like shit," Mitchell muttered next to him.

"I'd say all things considered," O'Conner offered, "you look quite good."

On the computer screen, Mitchell began to shake and twitch with increased intensity. The lights flickered.

Mitchell leaned in, staring at the screen intently now. Evans was sure that in spite of seeing the evidence before her, it would be hard for her to believe what she was about to see. Hell, it was hard for him to believe it.

"What do you see, Nicole?" the Evans in the video asked.

Here it was. Mitchell slowly leveled her head and locked eyes with Evans, who was just to the left of the camera. The lights flickered again in the video.

"*Derelinquas nos esse. Non venimus ad te,*" said Mitchell in the video.

Sitting next to him, Mitchell brought a hand up to her mouth. Her eyes were wide with shock.

The Evans in the video asked, "What did you say?"

Again, Mitchell repeated the strange phrase, her voice still unnaturally deep even through the tiny speakers. Evans leaned in. Something about those words seemed familiar, but he couldn't place it. In the moment, he'd been too focused on Mitchell's wellbeing. Now that she was safely sitting next to him and out of her hypnotic state, his mind felt free to focus on these strange words. That is, focus as well as he could given just how damn tired he was. He desperately wanted to sleep. He pushed the thought of sleep from his mind for the moment and waited to hear the words again.

"Nicole," the video Evans said, "focus. Hear my voice."

The screen went black as the video captured the moment when the lights went out completely. A split second later, the screen filled with multi-color digital blocks. The sound became choppy and distorted. Something was wrong!

"What the hell happened?" O'Conner asked.

Just as quickly as it came, the glitches or interference in the video cleared. The screen still dark, what little could be seen continuously blurred and sharpened as the little camcorder had desperately searched for anything to focus on in the darkness.

"... count back from ten and you are going to wake up," Evans's voice came from the speakers suddenly. "Ten."

"*Derelinquas nos esse! Non venimus ad te!*" The barely visible shape of Mitchell on the computer screen screamed.

Mitchell stood suddenly, moving away from the computer screen. Her hand still covered her mouth. Glancing back, Evans could see tears welling up in her eyes, but she stared at the screen nonetheless from where she stood now.

Looking back at the computer, Evans tapped the spacebar. The video stopped. He stared off into space, lost in thought as he tried to pinpoint what seemed familiar about those words.

"I don't remember that," Mitchell said. "I remember the exam table and the grey beings. But I don't remember yelling. What did I say?"

Evans looked back at her. He could see the terror in her eyes. She now had the memories—if they were indeed memories—that had surfaced during the hypnosis. But she, like Stephanie, had said something she had no memory of saying. Just what was going on here? Evans turned back to the computer and hit the spacebar again. The video continued.

From the speakers emitted the deep and distorted voice supposedly belonging to Mitchell screaming out that strange phrase again. Evans pounced on the spacebar. Silence returned to the room. The two women stared at him as his jaw dropped and recognition washed over him.

"It's Latin," he whispered.

He glanced over at Mitchell.

Mitchell shook her head and said, "I don't know Latin."

"But I used to," he said. "Catholic preparatory school. My Latin is rusty, but ..."

He pulled up a web browser on the laptop and punched in a search for a Latin to English translator. Finding one, he poised his fingers over the keys.

"Let me see," he muttered. "derelinquas."

He tapped out the word, "derelincuas." Then shaking his head, he hit the backspace key several times and tried again. "Derelinquas" with a Q. Slowly, he continued the process of typing out the words of the phrase Mitchell had said several times. Finally, he reached the end.

He hit enter and stared at the screen. The translation read, "Leave us be. We will not come to you." O'Conner and Mitchell leaned in close now to stare at the screen with him.

"What the hell does that mean?" O'Conner said.

"Latin is a bit tricky," Evans said. "It doesn't work exactly like English. It's been a long time since I've even thought about it. But I think it's a warning."

"A warning?" Mitchell frowned, still staring at the screen.

"Yeah," Evans pointed. "'Leave us be.' That part is pretty straight forward. The next phrase is a little tricky. The present tense and past tense can be hard to figure out, especially with so little context. But I think the point is, they're not interested in you."

He looked at Mitchell now. "You're not their target," he said.

"Or maybe you're not," she sighed. "Doesn't matter, I guess. Point is, we know who their target is. But they have us cornered now. I don't think we have any way of stopping them."

Even as fatigued as he was, Evans couldn't help but make the observation that both he and Mitchell were now talking about "them" as if they might actually believe aliens were behind all of this. Or maybe it was that he was coming around to Mitchell's theory that there was someone behind this? He had to admit this was getting incredibly bizarre.

Mitchell pressed her lips together and shook her head, her eyes still locked on the screen. Sighing again, she turned and jerked the door open and walked out of the room. Evans looked over at O'Conner. He hated to admit it, but Mitchell was right. They were in no better position now to stop these monsters—of whatever kind they might be—than they had been before. And now, Mitchell was flooded with disturbing visions of an alien abduction that may or may not have actually happened. But either way, the emotional scars it ripped open were nonetheless quite real. Guilt washed over Evans. It was followed by sheer exhaustion. All of a sudden, he was consumed with a desire to fall asleep as much out of fatigue as out of a desperate longing to escape the horrible weight of his guilt.

Forcing himself to his feet, he gathered his things. He and Mitchell had to get back to the motel. And then ... who the hell knew?

MITCHELL DROVE. HER EYES felt dry. Her body ached all over. She desperately wanted to shower, but knew she lacked the energy. Her hair felt disgusting. A slight taste of bile still lingered in her mouth.

Evans sat in the passenger seat. They drove in silence for several minutes; the motel wasn't far. She pulled the car into the parking lot of the motel and turned it off. For a moment, neither of them moved. Finally, Evans looked over at her.

"Are you okay?" he asked.

"Just need sleep," she said, looking straight ahead.

She swung open her door and unbuckled her seatbelt. As she got out of the car, Evans followed. They both slammed their doors shut. The sound echoed off the building. In the sky, the glow of a new day could be seen. But Mitchell wanted just to close her eyes, just to forget the day that had happened. She moved to her door.

"If you need anything ..." Evans said.

"Yeah," she said dismissively before he could say anymore. She wasn't in the mood for any of this. She just wanted to be alone.

"Nicole," Evans said, his voice low. "I'm sorry. I should not have done the hypnosis. I should have just ..."

"I told you to do it," she said flatly as she looked at him. "You were just doing what I asked you to do. There's nothing to apologize for."

Evans opened his mouth, but stopped short of saying anything else. He seemed worn out. His shoulders dropped a little. His eyes were more than just tired. They were apologetic, moving over the sight of her with pity and sorrow. No, he wasn't just tired, he seemed defeated. But she had nothing left inside of her in that moment to deal with him.

"Good night, Evans," she said.

Turning to her door, she plunged her key into the lock and opened it. She never looked back. She crossed the threshold, pulled the key from the door, and closed it behind her. Once inside, she looked at the door carefully. She threw the deadbolt, then she placed the chain.

Leaning her head against the door, she felt the tears come. With her complete exhaustion came now an inability to hold in any of her emotions. Her legs gave out and she slowly crumpled to the floor. There she lay, weeping. She wasn't sure how long she laid there, but eventually, she managed to move herself to the bed. She removed none of her borrowed clothes. She did not pull the covers back on the bed;

she merely curled up in a tight ball. She had cried herself to sleep before, but never like this.

CHAPTER THIRTEEN

SOMEWHERE IN THE DARK haze that was her mind, the ding of her cell phone receiving a text registered, but it wasn't nearly enough to rouse Mitchell from her fretful sleep. Her body's exhaustion dragged her into a deep sleep against her mind's will. Her mind, unsure how to process the events of the past nights, replayed nightmarish visions over and over: black eyes, grey hands with long fingers reaching out, instruments with sharp points, black eyes carefully taking in every inch of her body.

It might have been a moment later or an hour later, but her phone rang now. She stirred in bed. The last nightmare suddenly evaporating like an exhaled breath on a cold day. She fought the weight of her own body which still needed more sleep. She got up and found her bag by the door. Her phone was in it, still ringing. Picking it up, she answered without looking. Her eyes were too unfocused still to bother with trying to see who was calling.

"This is Agent Mitchell," she managed in a hoarse voice.

"Mitchell, this is Assistant Director Reynolds," said a stern male voice on the other end. "I just got off the phone with the North Woodstock Chief of Police. He's not exactly pleased with what's been going on up there."

She swallowed what little saliva she had in her already dry mouth and said, "I can explain everything. It will all be in my case report."

"No it won't," Reynolds said flatly. "You pack up right now and get back to Boston!"

She felt suddenly dizzy. Breathing became difficult, as if the air was being sucked from the room. "Sir, please, let me explain."

"You can explain when you report to me in person tomorrow."

What could she do? Everything was falling apart, but she could stop this. She still felt sure of that. "Sir, I need more time. I am close to catching whoever is doing this! I know he's going to strike in the next 24 hours."

She heard the Assistant Director sigh on the other end. She looked over at a sliver of sunlight that was managing to cut through a slight gap between the drawn curtains. Dust in the room swirled in that little shaft of light. It faded a little as a cloud somewhere far off came between her and the sun.

"Nicole," the Assistant Director said, "I know you've been through a lot. I really do. But I shit you not, if you don't get back to Boston right now I won't have any choice but to fire you. It's out of my hands. With everything going on, there are already too many eyes on the Bureau, particularly in Boston, you hear me? Don't do anything stupid. Don't draw any more attention to our department. You're hanging by a very tiny thread as it is. Just go get that damn shrink you dragged along with you and the two of you get back right now!"

The shaft of light was completely gone now. She stared down at the spot of the red carpet where it had been. "Okay," she managed to say through her clenched throat. A fresh tear travelled down her cheek, tickling its way to the corner of her mouth.

"I'll see you tomorrow," Reynolds said with a little more gentleness.

The line went dead.

Mitchell blinked back more tears and looked down at the phone. Sure enough, a text had come in. But she'd missed it. It had been from Anthony. It read, "What's going on? Asst. Dir. is pissed!!!"

So apparently word was getting around. She was a liability now. The Bureau wouldn't let that slide. She could hear it already, allegations that she was unstable and should not have been allowed back to work so soon. They would question everything Evans had done in his therapy sessions with her. They might even do all they could to discredit Evans. They needed someone to blame; it was better to blame an outsider. She'd fucked this up beyond her worst nightmares. She could see it already. If she indeed wasn't yet fired, she at least was officially no longer a field agent. She'd have a nice safe desk job tucked away somewhere. Maybe she'd get to make phone calls to forensic accountants who were investigating the shady dealings of some of the larger financial institutions on the East Coast. Or maybe they'd have her combing through files on hard drives in order to locate sensitive information from apprehended suspects. At any rate, she would never be out in the field again, that she was sure of.

And Evans ... she just hoped she could make sure they forgot about him.

She tossed the phone on her bed. It was running low on battery. But she could charge it in the car on their way home. She stopped suddenly at this thought. Am I really giving in to this? Am I really just going home now? But what choice did she have? What did she really have to go on that could stop all of this from happening?

She sat on the corner of the bed, her whole body feeling heavy.

Her legs and arms still ached as if she'd overexerted them recently. She sighed, thinking. *What if I just leave now and Stephanie is taken?* Could she really live with this? She had felt so certain that being kidnapped last night was a monumental blunder on the part of whomever was behind all of this. She thought for sure the hypnosis would have led to some significant insight. Instead, it had become a waking nightmare that now followed her about like a lingering dark cloud that not only blocked all light from her, but made everything somehow heavier.

Another frightening thought attacked her now: *What if I'm wrong about all of this? What if Stephanie is not taken? What if Evans is right and Stephanie just needs professional psychiatric help?* She would most definitely lose her job if she stayed and nothing at all happened. But she pushed those nagging thoughts from her mind. Something had definitely happened to her last night. That was real! How could she possibly doubt Stephanie's story now? How could she doubt it after last night's events?

So, what? I believe in aliens now? She shook her head, trying to shake off this new nagging thought. Every option before her seemed to lead to a dead end. How had she gotten in so deep, gotten so tangled up in this mess? When she was seventeen, she'd taken a dive into a deep dark pool from a high platform at night. She had been with some friends. In a effort to assert her independence and adventurous spirit, she was the first to take the dive from the thirty-foot platform. She went in feet first. But the angle of her body entering the water and the force of the impact twisted her about as she plunged deep into the dark water. The water had been incredibly cold. She had flailed her arms as she fell from the thirty-foot platform in an attempt to keep her body upright. When she hit the water, the underside of her arms smacked the water with an incredible force. Even as her body was driven into the water, the skin on her arms was stung sharply. Beneath the surface, in pain and disoriented, she panicked. Which way was up? How could she get back to the surface? That's how she felt sitting there in the motel room now. Which way was up? Which option made sense? Would she come out of this alive?

She pushed it all from her mind and focused on this moment. What could she do now? She could shower.

Standing, she shed the layers of borrowed clothing O'Conner had provided to her. Naked, she walked to the bathroom. She stopped, however, in front of the full length mirror on the wall next to the bathroom door. She stood there, looking at herself. Her hair was an awful tangled mess. She couldn't recall when it had looked this bad. Her body seemed weighed down, as if it had aged unnaturally overnight. On her stomach and ribs was the old familiar scar, but now she felt somehow detached from her own body as she stood there. Something had happened to her. And now, it was as if this thing, her own body, wasn't even hers any more. Her hands balled up into tight fists. What did they do to me?

A dark image entered her mind. She stood in her uniform before two naked men tied to a wooden beam. As she circled them, looking them up and down with contempt, she could feel the shame and hatred. Their bloodshot glaring eyes followed her as she circled. She had found no specific pleasure in their nakedness other than their total humiliation. If they weren't going to talk, they could deal with the humiliation ... and another long waterboarding session. As she circled, the patched up wound on her torso hurt. She liked that it hurt. It kept her from forgetting what these men had done, but there was a moment, when she made eye contact with one of the men as her eyes had traveled up his battered body. For a split second, she saw a wounded and shamed man, a violated man.

Standing there looking at her own naked body recalling what she'd experienced through the hypnosis, she felt her stomach turn. Looking into the reflection of her eyes, she didn't see her own eyes any more. She saw only that man's eyes, frozen in that moment of violation and shame.

She looked away, replacing the shame with the only feeling that felt powerful enough, the only feeling that felt right, self-hatred. Then a thought occurred to her. Did she have any marks? Like Tommy and Stephanie, had any marks been made on her body? She returned to the mirror and reached up to run her hand on the back of her neck. She felt nothing there. She ran her hands about around her jaw, down her neck, around her breasts—which were also sore, a common occurrence among female alien abductees, she noted—and down her side to her hips.

She felt something. Bumps protruded from her skin. She twisted around to look at her waistline at her right lower back. Something was there. Her heart raced now. This can't really be happening, she protested. She drew closer to the mirror, hardly able to breathe. Finally, she managed to look at what was on her skin. There were two bumps alright, one larger than the other. She ran her fingers over them. Finally, she sighed with frustration and relief. They were insect bites. They looked nothing like the distinct marks that had been found on Tommy and Stephanie.

She stepped back from the mirror and laughed at herself. You're really losing your goddamn mind, girl! She forced a laugh again. Then tears came to her eyes. Wiping them away, she stepped into the bathroom and threw on the shower. She stared at the falling water as the steam slowly began to fill the small bathroom. She just stared for a long time before stepping in. And even then, she just stood there for a very long time. She was only brought out of this state when she noticed blood mingling with the water on the shower floor. Looking down, she realized the blood trailed down her body. Touching her face, she found where it came from. Her nose was bleeding.

MITCHELL STEPPED OUT OF the door to her motel room. The air was humid given the previous day's rain. The temperature had quickly risen as well, so the slight breeze that confronted her outside was dense with humidity. It was late in the day already. Almost a whole day had passed. She'd slept for quite some time. She now wore dark wash jeans and a short sleeve grey shirt. She had applied minimal make-up, wishing only to mask the dark rings under her eyes. Beyond that, she felt no desire to waste her time and what little energy remained. She would just be driving with Evans back to Boston. Then she'd go home. And then what?

She stepped up to Evans's door. How would she tell him? How would he take it? If they left now, they'd likely hit traffic around Boston. At least they would be headed against the general flow of traffic as they would be headed into the city while most people would be headed out at the end of the day. All the same, she still faced more than two hours in the car, alone with Evans. And she was sure he'd want to talk about her situation, though she wasn't exactly sure she was ready to talk about it. But what other choice did she have? She stared at the door and took a deep breath.

She raised her hand, about to knock, when she felt fingers grasp her right shoulder. In her mind, all she could see was the image of one of those creature's lanky grey hands with cold long slender fingers and it made her skin crawl. It was only a split second, but it was enough to completely shake her. She whirled about, heart racing, ready for a fight, ready to take this thing down where it stood. She was blind with rage and fear.

"I'm sorry," came Diego's voice. "I didn't mean to scare you."

She blinked and her eyes focused on the man standing there, right hand still raised where he had touched her on her shoulder. He lowered it slowly, his wide eyes fixed on her. He seemed nearly as startled as she was. He also looked quite worn out. His hair was matted down and oily. What had he been up to?

"I asked Chief Wilson where I could find you," Diego said. "We need to talk."

EVANS HAD BEEN SITTING on the bed, laptop open, notebook out, pouring over notes again. He'd gotten up several hours ago, showered, walked to a nearby convenience store and grabbed something to eat. After last night, he didn't want to disturb Mitchell. He figured when she was ready to pick things up again, she would get him. But the day wore on. He took a break from the case, walked the short distance to the town. He explored the small park next to the river that ran through North Woodstock. The whole time, he kept checking his phone, wondering when she might call him. When she didn't, he ducked into the Chinese restaurant across from the tavern and grabbed more food to go. He returned to his dank motel room, ate, and began looking over his notes again, making new notes, new speculations, trying to make sense of what had happened last night. That was what he was doing when he heard a knock on his door.

Now he stood next to Mitchell. They looked at Diego who sat in the one chair in the room. The man appeared to have had his own long night and day. Evans wondered if he'd even been home.

"Thank you for seeing me," Diego said softly in his accent. "I didn't know for sure who to turn to at this point. I tried to talk to Stephanie's parents, but her father insists she has been through enough, that she is just a very sick girl who needs help. I think he just doesn't want to call any more attention to her, or to their family."

"What is it that you need?" Mitchell asked.

Evans noted that she stood with her arms crossed, feet squared up to Diego. She may have been dressed casually, but she was managing to step back into her familiar role as an authority figure. He wondered if this was comforting to her after last night. A good means to return things to normal. She kept her eyes locked on Diego.

"They visited me again last night," Diego said. "They're getting bold. They came right up to me this time."

Evans soaked in the man's body language. He sat with his hands resting on his thighs, shoulders slightly drooped forward, his eyes looking from Mitchell to Evans. They were tired but expectant eyes. *Is he telling the truth?*

"Where did this happen?" Mitchell continued in her even tone.

"Outside St. Jerome," Diego answered.

"What did they say?"

"Nothing. They just stared at me. I think they wanted to scare me," Diego said. Then smiling sheepishly, he added, "Well. They did scare me. They're taunting me."

"How so?" Mitchell asked.

"I believe," Diego began. "No, I feel it in my bones, in my lungs, in my heart. Just like when they appeared to me before Tommy was taken, I think they're telling me they're going to take Stephanie."

"But they didn't communicate with you?" Mitchell asked.

Evans noted a subtle change in her voice. *Was that surprise?*

Diego shook his head. "No. They didn't. They just stood there like before. But I had this horrible feeling ... still have this horrible feeling.

It was like they were there to intimidate me. There was one at first. Then two more joined the first. They did nothing. Yet, I can't help but feel the ... how do you say ... menace. It was like a wave of hatred that kept hitting me. And fear."

He brought his hands together and nervously cracked his knuckles. "I tried to see her," he said. "Stephanie. But the hospital will not let me. And like I said, her father doesn't want to draw any more negative attention to his daughter."

"What do you hope we can do?" Evans asked.

Diego tapped his fingers on his legs looking around the room. Was he working out what to say next or just how to say it? Evans watched him as he took a deep breath, held it for a second, then let it out slowly.

"I spoke with Chief Wilson," Diego said, at last. "He said you performed a hypnosis on Agent Mitchell last night."

Evans shot a glance over at Mitchell. She remained still, eyes on Diego, but he could see tension in her jaw and neck.

"I think we should do the same for Stephanie," Diego said.

Mitchell's eyes went wide, as did Evans's as he turned and looked at the man sitting before them. Could he be serious?

"And I want to help," Diego concluded softly.

Now this was out of left field. Evans knew that for most religious people, hypnosis appeared outside of their paradigm, that it was easier to simply denounce it wholesale. It was easier to comfortably stash it over in the imagined categorical box where they had tossed voodoo and witchcraft and other such things and never think of it again. But here was this man, a small town pastor, suggesting that he help them with the hypnosis of a young woman. Evans didn't know for sure what to do with this new information. What box of his own was he supposed to put Pastor Diego into? Possibly the Brazilian-born man who somehow became the pastor of a small church in a small town in

New Hampshire bucked the stereotypes for Latino and South American conservative religious types as well as the stereotypes for rural and small town Americana religious folk. Was he in fact part of some liberal denomination? Or was he none of these things and now playing some unexpected angle on them for his own purposes?

"Help?" Evans finally managed. "How?"

"We need to speak to Stephanie's mother," Diego explained. "If I advocate for hypnosis, I think she will allow it. Dorothy is the key to getting Tim to let the hypnosis happen. I believe I can talk Dorothy into supporting this."

Evans looked over at Mitchell who looked at him now for the first time since this conversation began. Her arms dropped to her side. She tried to hide it, but he could see how bewildered and conflicted she was. He felt it himself.

"We're running out of time," Diego pressed. "Please! I just want to help Stephanie before it's too late."

Mitchell turned her gaze to Diego. She looked at him for a moment before speaking. Finally, she said, "Let's go."

CHAPTER FOURTEEN

Tim Clark closed his eyes and sighed heavily. "Look," he said with a tone that did little to mask his annoyance. "I appreciate your concern, but we need to do what is best for our daughter. She's sick and needs medical help."

Mitchell sat forward in her seat in the Clark's living room, "Mr. Clark, with all due respect, how can you possibly believe that what has happened to Stephanie is strictly a matter of mental health?"

Next to her sat Evans. Next to him, in a folding chair Dorothy had brought from the kitchen, sat Diego. Tim and Dorothy were on the sofa. A small gap between them was where Stephanie might have been had she not been locked in a room inside a mental ward. Mitchell wondered if this was the ultimate reality of their marriage: a small yet definite gap between them at all times that was occupied by their one and only daughter.

"What evidence do you have there's even been a crime?" Tim pressed her. "That there's anything going on here other than that my poor daughter is sick?"

"Mr. Clark, I'm with you," Evans jumped in. "I'm a psychiatrist. I have treated many patients with a wide variety of difficult challenges. I sincerely believe most likely Stephanie is suffering from severe psychotic episodes or PTSD of some form. But people don't just develop those conditions. There has to be either a medical explanation or an emotional explanation."

"Emotional?" Dorothy asked, her voice soft, but the concern evident in her large eyes.

"Trauma," Evans explained. "Abuse of some sort she may be unable to remember as it is too painful to recall. So she may be repressing those memories. All I'm saying is that I want to help uncover whatever the source of all this is. As long as the source of Stephanie's problems remains a mystery, I doubt her condition will improve. I just want to help Stephanie."

To Mitchell's surprise, it wasn't Tim that asked the next question. Instead, Dorothy looked to Diego now and said softly, "And why do you want this?"

"Same reason," Diego answered. "Call it a hunch, gut feeling, the Holy Ghost. I believe these people were sent here to help Stephanie."

Mitchell noted that Diego did not divulge to them any details of his encounter the night before with the alien beings. Did he suspect they would throw him out? Call him crazy? Dismiss his idea of having Evans perform hypnosis on Stephanie? Was he lying to them? Or maybe lying to Mitchell and Evans? Or was it a calculated move on his part to simply achieve the result he wanted? Mitchell couldn't help but feel a sense of trepidation with this man. He seemed sincere enough, but something about the subtle choices he was making troubled her. *He has an angle, an agenda,* she said to herself. *But what choice do I have left?* Of course, she had the obvious choice of simply calling all of this off, taking Evans outside and explaining to him that she was off the case, thus, they were off the case. But in spite of her better judgment, here she sat.

Dorothy looked up at her husband. He sighed, glancing at her and then the floor. For such a tall man, he seemed small in that moment.

"I can remain in the room with Stephanie to watch over her," Diego said suddenly.

Mitchell looked over at him. She could see Evans was staring at him as well. This had not been part of their discussion earlier. What was the game this man was playing? Mitchell's mind raced, wondering if she'd just walked into some kind of scheme that Diego had laid out for them. If he had an angle after all, he was playing his cards now. She opened her mouth to say something, anything. But Dorothy beat her to it.

"I'd like that," she said, her voice soft, but the certainty of her tone unmistakable. Diego had won Dorothy over.

"Dorothy," Tim protested, "leave this to the doctors."

"What's the harm, Tim?" she said, looking up at her tall husband with resolute eyes. "If there's a chance we can get to the bottom of this, better now than later. Besides, Dr. Evans here is a doctor."

She reached out, across that gap between them, and placed her hand on his hand, which rested on his bony knee.

"I want my daughter back," she said.

Tim looked at his wife for a long moment. He nodded slowly. Turning his heavy eyes to Evans, he said, "Just this once. That's it!"

THE CAR CLIMBED THE slow curving road, its headlights cutting through the dwindling light of dusk. Mitchell sat behind the wheel. Evans looked out his window. Diego followed them in his truck. Mitchell glanced in her rearview mirror. The headlights coming from his truck felt bright to her eyes, even though it was not yet fully night. A dull ache behind her eyes and spreading through her skull persisted. At some point, she realized that it had been there for some time, possibly since she had been found last night. But with so much else going on, it had not registered. Now having slept and cleaned up, the ache rose to the surface. But more pressing than the headache was a question that nagged her mind.

"What's his angle?" she said.

Evans looked over at her. "Diego?"

"He didn't say he planned on being present during the hypnosis. Was this his goal all along? What does he want with all of this?"

"I don't know," Evans admitted. "I can't quite figure him out."

Mitchell glanced in the mirror again and said, "Do you think he can be trusted?"

Evans stared out the windshield, considering her question. At length, he said, "I honestly have no idea. But if he interferes with the hypnosis ..." He trailed off.

Mitchell glanced at Evans. He seemed rested, but it was clear that the last few days had taken a serious toll on him. She imagined that once he was back in Boston he would need more time to recover. Would he bother to clear his schedule again, or would he simply wish to return to his routine?

The thought of returning to her routine sucked any remaining joy from Mitchell. What routine? She would most likely be out on her ass, unless there was some serious breakthrough that would lead to the apprehension of those responsible for Stephanie's kidnappings—for her kidnapping—it was not likely that she would have a job when she got back to Boston. A nagging little voice in the back of her head pointed out to her, this isn't the movies. What are the chances you can wrap up the case neatly and be forgiven your insubordination? That's what she was doing, wasn't it? She was being insubordinate. She was directly defying the orders given to her by Assistant Director Reynolds.

Her entire body felt heavy. Her stomach turned slightly. She glanced over at Evans, who was lost in his own thoughts. He had no idea what she was doing. She felt a compulsion to blurt it out, to be honest with him. What would he do? Certainly, he would call off the hypnosis and demand they return to Boston immediately. But if he didn't know, he could be insulated from blame. It was entirely her doing.

She blinked, and in the split second of darkness, her mind saw those black eyes staring at her, those horrible hands reaching for her. Rage bubbled up in her heart. She felt so powerless. She might as well have been right back on that damn examination table, unable to move. But she shoved these thoughts aside with the determination that she now could and would fight back. There was nothing left to it now. After last night, it didn't seem possible to return to a routine, to any semblance of normality. She just wanted to gouge out those large black eyes with her bare hands.

"I'll need you to keep an eye on him," Evans said, pulling her out of her mental sinkhole.

"What?" she glanced at him. "Oh, Diego. Yeah. Sure thing."

"Are you okay?" Evans asked.

"Yeah," she said flatly.

"Nicole," he said more softly. "I'm worried about you. After what happened last night, I think you're going to need some time to process all of this."

"Yeah," she nodded, eyes on the road.

"I'm serious. You ... vanished last night. I can't even begin to make sense of that. I think we're in over our heads here. Maybe this is a bad idea."

"You're not starting to believe in aliens, are you doctor?" she said, allowing a little more harshness into her voice than she had intended. Maybe it was the nagging doubts in her own mind that caused her to be so repulsed by the idea. But it's ludicrous, she thought. There's a reasonable explanation. Giving into hysteria is not the answer.

"I'm not saying I believe in aliens," Evans replied, keeping his voice even. "I'm just saying that ... Nicole, you vanished last night and traveled a serious distance in a very short time. You screamed Latin at me. Something happened to you. I can't explain these things."

"I can't either," she said. "Yet. But that's no reason to abandon logic."

"I'm not suggesting we abandon logic," Evans retorted, not hiding his increasing agitation. "I'm just saying that we might be dealing with something we are not in a position to understand at the moment."

A small part of her mind registered his comment and even agreed with it. But where did that sentiment lead? Again, she felt her doubt rise. What if I have been blind to the facts of the case? What if Stephanie was really abducted by alien beings? What if I was abducted by aliens? What if it's all real? What do I expect to find by putting Stephanie under hypnosis?

She shoved all of these nagging questions aside. Something had definitely happened to her, and in time she would have to deal with it, but not tonight. The choice had been made, a course of action set in motion. Maybe she just desperately wanted to prove she was right, that there was, in fact, someone behind this alien absurdity. But one thing was certain: she could not walk away now.

"We just need to keep Stephanie from being taken tonight," she said, increasing her foot's pressure on the gas pedal.

STEPHANIE SAT ON HER bed. She wore a hospital gown as before. Her hair was tangled, her skin pale and oily. Dark circles were under her eyes. Even in the short time since Evans had first met her, she seemed to have lost weight. Judging from the untouched tray of food that sat on the small table by the bed, she was not eating. Maybe it was the drugs. Maybe it was the trauma.

Evans pulled up a chair and set his messenger bag next to it. Mitchell finished setting up the camcorder they had borrowed from the North Woodstock Police. Diego was in the hallway with Tim and Dorothy Clark.

"Stephanie," Evans began, "Do you remember me?"

She nodded.

"I'm going to try to help you,' he said. "We have talked to your parents and ..."

"And you're going to hypnotize me," she cut in. "They told me."

She seemed almost stoic given everything she'd been through the last few days.

"That's right," Evans nodded. "Now, I know it can be frightening to remember some of these things. But it's important for us to confront this so we work through it. We are going to be here with you the whole time. You're safe. Nothing bad is going to happen to you. Okay?"

She nodded, looking off.

"We're ready," Evans said to Mitchell.

She moved to the door and stepped into the hallway. Evans took this opportunity to stand himself and step outside the room. He watched as Mitchell informed the Clarks and Diego that they were ready. They all nodded. Diego excused himself from their conversation and moved towards Evans. The Clarks watched him go.

"I'll come get you when we're done," Mitchell said to the Clarks.

Dorothy shot a quick pleading glance to Evans. He nodded to

her, hoping it communicated his sincere desire to help Stephanie. The Clarks turned and walked down the hallway towards the waiting area.

As Mitchell and Diego approached the door, Mitchell reached out and firmly grabbed Diego by the arm, stopping him.

"Didn't tell us you'd be in here," she said firmly in a soft voice so it wouldn't carry down the hall.

Diego smiled. "Would you have allowed it otherwise?"

"I swear if you interfere at all ..."

"I'm only here to help," Diego interrupted Mitchell's threat. "And at the moment, I'm the only reason this is happening. Please, Agent Mitchell. If nothing else, have a little faith in me."

She let go of his arm and Diego walked into the room. Mitchell followed him. Evans, still standing by the door, shot Mitchell a quick look as she passed him. Here goes nothing, he thought.

Walking in, he pulled the door closed behind him. It clicked loudly as it closed.

Diego walked to the far wall of the room. He stood in the corner, left hand over right, in a comfortable stance and said nothing. Mitchell stood next to the camcorder on the flimsy tripod. Evans moved to the chair that sat across from Stephanie. She watched the three of them, but said nothing.

"Stephanie, I'm going to ask you to lay down," Evans said.

She complied, laying on her back.

Evans walked her through his initial instructions for the hypnosis. She said nothing, but nodded at times to indicate she understood what he was saying. At last, Evans began the process, asking her to close her eyes, relax, and breathe deeply. He began the countdown.

At three, Stephanie took in a deep breath, then let it out slowly. At zero, she took a sharp breath and her eyes shot open. But she remained on the bed. Her eyes stared vacantly up at the ceiling.

"Where are you, Stephanie?" Evans asked.

"In my bedroom," she said softly. "It's night."

"Are you alone?"

"No," she said, her voice now in a higher pitch. She shook slightly.

"Who is with you?"

"I can't see them. But I can feel them ... watching ... waiting."

"Waiting for what?"

Stephanie let out a short cry of terror. Her hands gripped the sheets on her bed.

"What's happening, Stephanie?"

"It's the light," she said, fighting to keep control of her wavering voice. "It's coming for me. They're taking me. I don't want to go! I don't want to go again!"

Her body twitched and twisted slightly as she seemed to fight some invisible force.

"Where are they taking you?"

"I'm in the ship," she said. "On some kind of table. No, no, no. Don't touch me! Leave me alone!"

"What are they doing?"

"They're examining me. I don't want them to touch me."

"How many are there?" Evans asked.

"Three of them," she said.

She screamed again and her body contorted.

"Stephanie, what's happening?"

"No, no, no," she cried out. "They're putting things inside of me. There's a needle. It's so long. They're ... taking my eggs. They say they need them."

Evans glanced back at Mitchell to see how she was handling this having just been through her own similar hypnosis last night. She stared at Stephanie with no expression on her face. Her poker face, he thought. Turning back to Stephanie, he carried on.

"Why do they need your eggs?" he asked.

Tears ran down Stephanie's cheeks as she stared off into infinity, laying there on her back. "To build a new race," she said with a choked voice. "To save humanity. To save us from ourselves."

TIM AND DOROTHY SAT in the waiting area. Tim held Dorothy's small hand in his. Through the front doors of St. Jerome, Chief Wilson burst in. A gust of hot and humid summer air flowed through the door. He was followed by Agent Anthony Brown. Chief Wilson spotted the Clarks immediately.

"Is it true?" he barked, "You let that quack and FBI agent perform a hypnosis?"

"What's it to you?" Dorothy shot back, much to Tim's surprise.

"Well, according to Agent Brown here with the FBI," Wilson indicated the man in the suit next to him. "Agent Mitchell was told to drop this case and return to Boston this afternoon."

"That little ..." Tim stood.

Dorothy reached out and grasped his hand as he stood. "It's okay, Tim."

"What do you mean, it's okay?" He shot back at her.

Dorothy stood up, looking at Wilson and Brown. "If it's all the same to you," she said in a soft but firm voice, "the hypnosis is underway already and I'd like it to be carried out in full."

Wilson sighed, shaking his head. "Dorothy, we've known each other a long time. But I gotta' ask, are you sure about this?"

She nodded.

"Just to be clear," he added. "That FBI agent in there has gone against direct orders from her superiors. If there's any criminal case here at all, it is within my jurisdiction at this point."

Dorothy nodded again. "You'll have your jurisdiction and you can deal with Agent Mitchell as you all see fit when the hypnosis is over. But I'm asking you, please, let them finish what they have already started."

Wilson shrugged looking over at Agent Brown. Brown raised his eyebrows and shook his head.

"I can't believe it," Brown muttered. "Son of a bitch."

CHAPTER FIFTEEN

Cold sweat covered Stephanie now. Mitchell watched as the girl jerked her head to one side then another. Her hands still gripped the sheets of her bed. Her feet twitched and spasmed. Mitchell periodically glanced over to Diego. He'd stood almost completely still so far. His eyes remained focused on Stephanie and didn't wander at all.

"It's okay," Evans said to Stephanie. "We're right here. Can you tell us what's happening?

Stephanie arched her back on the bed and her legs kicked. A suppressed cry of pain leaked from her throat. She collapsed back on the bed, breathing hard.

"They're putting more implants in me!" she said. "In my back."

She writhed again. Evans leaned closer. He spoke softly, probably in an effort to be as soothing as possible.

"Stephanie, listen to me," he said. "I need you to focus on the beings in the room."

"I can't," she said through tears.

"I need you to try," Evans gently pressed her.

"No. I can't do it!"

"Listen to me carefully," Evans continued softly. "They can't hurt you anymore. You're safe."

"No one is safe," Stephanie shot back in a hoarse whisper.

Mitchell glanced over at Diego again. She noticed now that the man's mouth was moving. What was he doing? She could not hear any words from him, but his mouth was definitely moving, forming words quickly, continuously.

"Why is no one safe?" Evans asked.

Stephanie turned her head to one side then the other. Again, she arched her back. It looked painful to Mitchell. The young woman was clearly exerting incredible force to do that.

"Tell him to stop that," Stephanie said, her voice strained as she arched her back.

Evans looked around, confused. He looked to Mitchell and she shrugged, unsure of what to make of this. She looked at Diego, though, and noticed he still remained focused on Stephanie. His mouth moved quickly. It was as if he were silently chanting. Looking at Evans, Mitchell nodded her head over to Diego. Evans glanced over at him.

"Tell who to stop what?" Evans tried.

"Tell him to stop that," Stephanie said again, her voice rising in pitch, caught somewhere between a plea and a demand.

"Who? Diego?" Evans asked.

Now Mitchell could hear Diego. His words were unintelligible, but he was definitely murmuring something. Stephanie collapsed on the bed, her back no longer arched. Her hands relaxed, letting go of the sheets. Slowly, she craned her head up to look at Diego. It was an unnatural movement, her whole body relaxed but her neck forced up oddly with such tension. Something about it unsettled Mitchell as she watched this. Stephanie's eyes locked on Diego, who still stood in the corner.

"TELL HIM TO STOP THAT!" Stephanie screamed so loud, everyone in the room jumped. Mitchell's headache instantly increased.

Evans sat back, startled. Mitchell shook where she stood. What is happening? In her bewilderment, it took a moment for it to register that Mitchell now heard a man's voice speaking. It was Diego. He'd increased the volume of his chanting.

"... on Earth as it is in Heaven," Diego recited. "Give us this day our daily bread and forgive us our sins as we forgive those who sin against us. And lead us not into temptation, but deliver us from evil ..."

It was as if a bomb went off in the room. Stephanie screamed at a piercing decibel. It happened so fast, but the onslaught of fear and adrenaline gave Mitchell just enough of an ability to soak in the events that happened simultaneously. The lights in the room flickered and went out. They were plunged into darkness. Only a shaft of yellow light from a lamp post outside cut through the window. Stephanie's scream was long and unnatural, an inhuman howl of hatred and pain. Mitchell's head throbbed now. Evans was white, eyes wide.

"What's happening?" Mitchell yelled.

Diego now yelled out his words, "Jesus Christ my lord, grant me your power and authority in this battle."

Mitchell stared in shocked disbelief at the man. He was screwing it all up. What was he doing? He was ruining the only chance they had left to help Stephanie. "What's he doing?" she demanded of Evans.

Evans looked over at Diego, face still white. But some kind of recognition washed over him in that moment. "Let him," he said. "Let him do it!"

Stephanie sat up in her bed. She cocked her head far to the left and glared at Diego. Mitchell had never seen so much hatred in someone's eyes before. It was as if a wave of heat coming from a large fire swept out over the room, but this heat was pure disdain. Stephanie opened her mouth and spoke, but it was not Stephanie's voice. It was deep, guttural, raspy, distorted. Every syllable made Mitchell's skin crawl.

"She's ours, Pastor Diego Silva *de Corumba!*" she said in that other voice, then smiled with her lips only. Her eyes remained unchanged daggers of loathing.

"In the name of Christ Jesus, be silent demon!" Diego responded, not breaking eye contact with this hideous version of Stephanie.

Stephanie responded, but Mitchell could not understand what she said. *"Eu te conheço muito bem, Deigo Silva. Você não está pronto para brincar com nosso fogo."*

"No nome de Jesus Cristo, eu ordeno que você libere essa garota!" Diego replied.

It took Mitchell a moment to realize that this girl from New Hampshire was speaking perfect Portuguese to the Brazilian man in the corner. What the hell is happening? She felt light headed. The pain in her head was now a constant sharp pressure.

Evans, still seated, but watching this exchange in complete shock, reached down to his bag. Pulling out his notebook, he retrieved the crucifix necklace and tossed the notebook aside. He stood quickly and moved to Stephanie. He placed the crucifix in front of Stephanie's face.

Stephanie slowly cocked her head all the way over to the other side and glared up at Evans. Her expression changed as she looked at him. It wasn't hatred anymore. It was almost as if she were amused, in the most sinister manner possible, by Evans's gesture.

"You come at me with your meaningless trinket," Stephanie spat at Evans in that dark voice. "Your mother would be ashamed, Alan."

"Stephanie. Listen to me," Evans said. "I need you to come back."

"Oh she's not coming back," Stephanie smirked at him.

He thrust the crucifix closer to her. In a swift move, she grabbed his hand and bit down on it. Evans yelled in pain. She let go and he pulled his arm back.

She lunged at Evans with incredible force. They hit the ground. Mitchell was sure she heard Evans's head hit the floor hard. Stephanie bit down on his neck now, drawing blood. Evans screamed in pain. Mitchell stared in disbelief, hardly able to move.

"Get her off him!" Diego yelled as he jump forward and pulled on Stephanie's arm.

Mitchell still stared, unable to move.

"Agent Mitchell, HELP ME!" Diego screamed at her.

Snapping out of her state of complete shock, Mitchell grabbed Stephanie's other arm. Despite how thin her arm was, it felt as if Mitchell were trying to haul a linebacker off of Evans. She pulled with all her might.

"In the name of Christ Jesus, I command you to get off him!" Diego yelled at Stephanie.

Suddenly, Stephanie became much lighter. They practically threw her against the wall with the sudden change in weight. Evans scurried back, and assessed his wounds. Both Diego and Mitchell managed to keep a hold of the flailing girl. They pressed her against the wall as she fought to be released. She stopped suddenly, though. Looking at Mitchell now, Stephanie smiled that menacing and unnatural smile, Evans's blood on her teeth. Mitchell wanted to throw up. Her head swam in a sudden onslaught of dizziness. What is happening to me? Stephanie chuckled, if it could really be called that. It was more of a guttural rattle and clicking that emitted from her throat. She showed her teeth in a mock smile and clicked them together.

"Hello again, Nicole," Stephanie said in that deep growl of a voice.

Terror swept through Mitchell. She wanted to run and hide. It was as if she were on that examination table again. Stephanie's eyes were dilated, blood shot, and filled with hate. Blood dripped from the corner of her mouth. For a split second, Mitchell felt as if she were about to faint. The room spun around her. When she tried to look at Stephanie again, she found she was holding not a young woman, but a hideous grey alien against the wall. It s large back eyes bore into her mind.

Mitchell screamed and let go of the thing. But even as she did this, she realized it was only Stephanie. Diego fought to keep her against the wall, but she was strong.

"Don't let go!" he yelled. "No matter what happens, don't let go. Don't let it get in your head. Don't listen to it."

Mitchell stepped forward and resumed her post, holding Stephanie against the wall. Someone was at the door now. They were trying to open it. Apparently they were unsuccessful. They have the keys, Mitchell couldn't help thinking. Just open the door. But they remained unable to do so. They banged on the door and demanded that it be opened. Mitchell recognized the exasperated voice of Chief Wilson. They banged again, demanding that they stop what they were doing and open the door immediately.

For a moment, Mitchell felt the impulse again to run and hide. Just let them in. Let me out of here! But she stood her ground. Could this really be happening? Or was it like Evans had suggested in his book and lecture? Stephanie's mind was just so convinced in this moment that she was possessed that she was manifesting such symptoms? Possession? Mitchell couldn't even bring herself to accept that possibility. But some horrible sense of foreboding swirled in her gut. Something about all of the hatred and fear that almost visibly flowed out of Stephanie made Mitchell feel certain that something much deeper and darker than a mental illness or twisted manifestation of post traumatic stress was in that room with her. And all she wanted to do was run out of that room, run as far as she possibly could. She never wanted to see one of those hideous aliens again.

"Give me that!" Diego yelled over his shoulder to Evans, who was still on the floor. "Give me the crucifix!"

Evans grabbed the crucifix that had fallen to the floor during Stephanie's animal-like attack. He got up and handed it to Diego who snatched it. Diego pressed the crucifix into Stephanie's forehead. Her eyes rolled into the back her head, becoming nothing more than bloodshot whites. She craned her head back against the wall, forcing her body to arch backwards away from it. She groaned and bloody drool rolled out of her mouth.

"In the name of the Father, the Son and the Holy Spirit," Diego commanded, "tell me how many of you there are!"

Stephanie hissed and began banging her head against the wall repeatedly. Mitchell had to lean in now to try to keep control of the girl. Her forearms burned with the effort. She'd fought to keep control of suspects before, but never anything like this. Stephanie's skin was hot, as if she were running a very high fever. There was so much sweat now that Mitchell's grip threatened to slip off.

"Demon, I will not allow you to hurt this girl!" Diego said angrily. "Tell me how many of you there are!"

Stephanie stopped hitting her head. Her eyes rolled back and she focused all of her otherworldly hatred on Diego.

"How many of us would you like there to be?" she said in a deep growl.

"In the name of Jesus Christ I command you to tell me how many of you there are!" Diego said firmly.

"Three. Two. One. Zero." Stephanie smiled that sick perversion of a smile.

She looked at Evans next, who stood back, holding his neck. Blood seeped through his fingers and ran down his dress shirt. Stephanie made that awful chuckling and clicking sound again as she tried to move towards him. Mitchell shoved her back. A sudden wave of anger washed over Mitchell. She'd had it. Whatever was happening here, she was sick of the fear. She wanted to hurt something. She wanted to make this all go away. She remembered why she was in that damn room in the first place.

"Where is Tommy Ferguson?" Mitchell said.

She glared at Stephanie. Or did she really believe that Stephanie was even there anymore?

"Still hung up on Tommy?" the voice asked through Stephanie's lips.

The rage took over Mitchell. "What did you do to him?" she screamed with all her might.

Stephanie cackled a horrible rasping laugh and pushed herself away from the wall in spite of how hard Diego and Mitchell fought to keep her there.

"Alan, help us!" Mitchell called out.

Evans stood back, watching in shock.

"On the bed," Diego cried out. "Get her to the bed!"

Shaken out of his shock, Evans jumped forward and helped them fight the unnaturally strong girl down to the bed. Evans held down her feet. Diego and Mitchell wrestled with her arms.

"Tell me where Tommy Ferguson is!" Mitchell demanded again.

"In the name of Jesus Christ, speak the truth!" Diego yelled. He glanced up at Mitchell and she caught just a glimpse in his eyes of something. He was trying to help her. "Speak the truth, you demons. By the blood of Christ, speak the truth!"

Stephanie's mouth opened unnaturally wide then closed. Finally, words formed. "Linden ... pond," said the hideous voice.

Mitchell looked back to Diego. That was it. An answer. Time to finish this! She nodded. He wasted no time.

"By the authority of Jesus Christ, whom I serve," he said firmly, pressing the crucifix to Stephanie's forehead. "I command every evil spirit within Stephanie to leave! Depart now and never come back!"

Stephanie's jaw dropped open again. She opened her mouth so far Mitchell was sure she would hear her jaw popping out of place any moment. A rasping growl came from her throat. It increased in volume steadily.

"Listen to me, you fowl things. In the name of Jesus Christ, the son of God, I command you to release Stephanie!" Diego yelled.

Stephanie's body convulsed. The growl morphed into a deafening howl of agony. The hair on Mitchell's arms stood at the sound. It was not one howl, it was three howls. Three voices screamed out as if simultaneously being tortured. The howl became a piercing scream that shook Mitchell's eardrums to the point that she thought for sure she would be deaf if she ever got out of that room.

Suddenly, Stephanie's body went completely limp. She lay on the bed and didn't move. Unsure of what was happening now, Mitchell kept her grip tight around Stephanie's right arm. Stephanie coughed suddenly, then looked around. When her eyes met Mitchell's, all that Mitchell saw now was a terrified girl.

"Stephanie?" Diego said softly.

"What's happening?" Stephanie said in a horse and shaken voice. But it was unmistakably her own voice again.

Diego let go. Taking their cue from him, Mitchell and Evans let go as well. They stood looking down at the very confused and frightened young woman.

"It's okay," Diego said. "Everything's okay now."

The lights in the room flickered and came on. Suddenly, those outside were able to open the door.

CHAPTER SIXTEEN

THE CLOUDS HAD CLEARED. Mitchell could see the stars outside over the tree tops and above the white mountains. She stood at a window in the waiting area of St. Jerome. Off in a corner, Diego sat with Stephanie, Tim, and Dorothy. She glanced over at the group. They had their hands together, heads bowed. Diego seemed to be leading them in a prayer.

The nurse on-duty finished patching up Evans's hand, having already cared for his neck. Nothing serious had been hurt, but the bite was strong and would likely leave a scar. Mitchell wondered how he'd explain that one to people. She turned back to the window and stared out. The headache was now a dull throbbing. Hopefully the painkillers she'd taken would be kicking in soon.

"Wanna' tell me what the hell happened here?" she heard Brown say behind her.

She turned and looked at him. When the door to the room had finally opened, he'd been right there with Chief Wilson. She'd known in that moment that it was over.

"I don't know if you'd believe me," she said turning back to the window.

"I tried to vouch for you," Brown said, stepping up to the window and standing next to her to look out. "Look ... there's no easy way to say this ..."

"Sure there is," Mitchell said softly. "I'm fired. I'm a loose canon, a liability. I went against direct orders from the Assistant Director."

Brown looked over, eyebrows raised. "Shit, that's almost what he said verbatim."

She turned to him now. "In five years, I've had the Assistant Director scold me enough."

"What are you gonna' do?"

She shrugged. "The real question is, what are you going to do? I have one last thing I need you to take care of for me."

Brown shook his head, raising his hands. "I can't. I was sent up here to get you. Chief Wilson ratted you out, I'm afraid. He called us up and said something happened to you last night. Are you okay?"

"I'm fine," she said, then added, "I think."

"What the hell happened? You were drunk?"

"Is that what Wilson said?"

"Said you and Dr. Evans had been drinking. And then ..." Brown searched for what to say next.

"That I was abducted by aliens?" Mitchell offered.

Brown looked at her, not exactly amused. "Is that what you'd call it?"

"I don't know what I'd call it," she said, looking out the window. "But something did happen to me, Anthony. Last night. And now, tonight."

She looked at him again and said softly, "That's why I need you to do just one more thing for me."

"I'll get into some deep shit," he shook his head.

"Listen to me," she leaned closer to him and whispered intensely. "I know where Tommy Ferguson's body is."

Brown's jaw went slack. "Are you serious?"

"Linden Pond," Mitchell nodded. "We're ... you're going to need a team. If you call them now, they can start searching in the morning."

Brown looked around the room, thinking this over. Mitchell knew it would be a pretty big gamble on his part to believe her now, but they'd known each other for five years. She felt sure he would do the right thing. He looked at her, clearly bewildered.

"Trust me," she said. "Call it in."

And with that, she walked away. She approached Evans, who was inspecting the bandage on his right hand which the nurse had just finished applying.

"You ready to go get a stiff drink?" Mitchell asked him.

"Or twelve," Evans replied.

"Not sure that's such a good idea," the male nurse chimed in.

"You're right," Evans nodded. "It's more like the best goddamn idea I've heard in years." He grinned up at Mitchell. "Come on. You're buying."

Standing, Evans headed for the door. Mitchell followed. But as she reached the door, she glanced back at Brown. He still stood by the window, looking in on the room. He watched her head for the door. She stopped there for a moment, wishing she knew what else to say to him. Some day she might be able to tell him about everything that had happened over the last three days, but not tonight. She just hoped he would, in fact, make the call. She tried to plead with him with her eyes.

Brown gave her a single nod. From his inside pocket in his suit jacket, he pulled out his cell phone. Mitchell turned and walked out of St. Jerome, hoping to never see the place again.

THE YELLOW TAPE FLUTTERED in the breeze. Several cars and two black vans were parked along the side of the road, including three police cruisers from North Woodstock and two more from Lincoln. The sun was up and the day was already quite warm, though thankfully not as humid as the day before. There were people everywhere, many in jackets with FBI printed in a large yellow font on their backs. They'd been pouring over the area around Linden Pond for nearly two hours. Search dogs barked in the distance.

Mitchell and Evans stood across the road leaning against Mitchell's car that sat just off the shoulder. They watched the work being done. Mitchell wondered if she should be there at all, but she had to know.

"I thought I'd find you here," Diego said as he approached them. He seemed in a much better state now. He must have gotten some good sleep, a nice shower, and probably a hearty breakfast. At least Mitchell knew that those were all things she'd needed that morning.

Mitchell and Evans looked over at him. He smiled at them and stopped next to them.

"I wanted to thank you both," he said.

"For what?" Mitchell asked. "I'm not sure I know what happened last night."

"It's a lot to take in," Diego nodded. "Trust me, I know. Oh!"

He reached into his pocket and pulled out the crucifix necklace that belonged to Evans. He held it out for Evans to take.

"I wanted to give this back to you," he said.

Evans regarded the crucifix, then slowly put out his hand. Diego dropped it into his open palm. Evans just looked down at it as if unsure of what to make of this strange item.

"It's not a magic trick, Dr. Evans," Diego said. "It's just a thing. But things can help us sometimes if a thing helps us remember a deeper truth we may have forgotten."

Evans looked up at Diego, uncertainty in his eyes. "Thank you," was all he managed to say as he closed his hand around the crucifix and placed it in his pocket.

Mitchell seized this opportunity to ask Diego the question that had come to her last night somewhere between her third or fourth drink. "Did you know all along?"

"Know?" Diego said, eyebrows up. "That Stephanie was possessed? Honestly, no."

"Then how?" Mitchell pressed.

Diego took a deep breath and let it out, a slight smile on his lips. "I hoped that under hypnosis, any such evils might be ... exposed. I've come face to face with these beings twice now. And both times ... I could not shake the sense of ... well, it's like they suck all of the joy and hope right out of you where you stand. All that's left is fear. A fear so complete, it's like a vast ocean of darkness created for one purpose: to swallow you whole. I think you know what I mean, Agent Mitchell."

She looked down at the ground taking in his words. Yeah, she knew what he meant, knew it all too well.

"If you ever need anything, please call me," Diego added. "I hope you believe me now that I only wish to help."

"Mitchell!" Brown called out from across the road. He was jogging up to the yellow tape. Ducking under it, he crossed to them.

"Now if you'll excuse me," Diego said to Mitchell and Evans. "I need to rest. You are both in my prayers."

Diego turned and walked back down the road towards his pick-up truck that was pulled off a little ways down close to one of the North

Woodstock Police cruisers. There were so many more questions Mitchell could have asked him. Who was this strange man, and why did he not indulge in preaching to them now that they'd experienced ... but what had they experienced last night?

"We found something," Brown said, slightly out of breath as he reached them.

"Tommy?" Mitchell asked.

"We'll have to run dental records," Brown said. "But ... state of decomposition seems right as well as the size."

Though Mitchell felt so much lighter on her feet today than she had last night, a invisible weight seemed to flow off of her upon hearing this. It was Tommy. She had no doubt about it. She didn't need the dental records. They'd found Tommy. They'd found him, and Stephanie had not vanished.

"I thought you should know," Brown said softly.

"Thanks," she said to her friend.

"Maybe with this, you can talk to the AD and—"

Mitchell just shook her head, which was enough to cut Brown off.

"Come on, you can't be serious?" Brown asked. "What are you going to do?"

"I don't know yet," Mitchell admitted. "But I think it's time for something new."

It surprised even her to hear the words come out of her mouth. But there was relief too in letting them slip out. What would she do now? She could see various options before her. She could end up getting some random job, though it wouldn't be all that exciting. She'd need to find a cheaper place to live, so she'd move. Growing restless, she'd find another job. She'd likely bounce around different jobs for the next three or four years. Or maybe she could move back closer to her mother. Did she really want to live in up-state New York again? Where else could she go? She had old friends on the west coast. It didn't matter right then. And somehow figuring out what to do next didn't concern her at the moment. She just shrugged.

"Shit," Brown smiled, "You're one tough nut to crack." He paused, looking at her sadly. "Going to miss you."

"Oh, I'll be around, I'm sure," she said.

Brown nodded. Reluctantly, he turned back and walked across the road. Back under the yellow tape. Back to work.

"So you're really moving on?" Evans asked her.

She looked over at him and said softly, "What the hell happened last night?"

"I don't know," he answered.

"Was that real?"

"Well, it was real to Diego and Stephanie at least."

She felt sure he'd say this. But something felt off about this to her. Maybe Evans hadn't felt the waves of hatred and fear that had emanated from Stephanie last night. He hadn't experienced what she experienced when she was taken, when she was hypnotized, when she looked into Stephanie's eyes last night. No, she told herself, those were not Stephanie's eyes last night.

"Alan, that thing knew you," she almost whispered. "It knew your mother gave you that crucifix. Stephanie talked to Diego in Portuguese. That's not just some kind of psychotic episode."

Evans looked down at the asphalt. He shrugged. He can't bring himself to believe it. It's too much. Hell, it's too much for me to even admit. But what choice is there left? I was wrong. Sort of. There was someone behind all of this. But not someone I could arrest.

"So you buy it?" Evans asked. "Demons?"

"I don't know," she said. Hearing it aloud like that brought back other doubts. What if she was wrong about that too?

Evans shook his head. "I left that world behind a long time ago. A world of angels and demons, virgin birth, resurrection from the dead. It's too convenient to blame all the evil of this world on unseen forces, some devil with a pitch fork going around and causing mischief and mayhem, fighting some cosmic battle. And even if such forces are real, what keeps them from destroying us at any moment?"

She looked out at the fluttering yellow tape that was stretched between trees and posts that had been temporarily driven into the ground. "Maybe there's two kinds of evil in the world," she said softly. "Maybe there's what we do to each other, and there's these things."

Everyone seemed to be headed off to the far side of the pond. That must be where the body was found. Why had they done this? He was just a boy. Why had this happened to Tommy and almost happened to Stephanie, but not to others? She fought for clarity amid the swirling questions, trying to express to Evans what was bouncing around in her mind.

"But if that kind of evil is real," she said. "There has to be good."

"God?" he asked.

"Maybe Diego calls it God. Maybe it's bigger than that one word could ever encompass."

She looked over at Evans. She could see him processing this. But she also knew that it went against his view of the world, a view that ran deep. A view, she suspected, might not leave a whole lot of room for things so far outside of the realms of science and medicine, and she understood. She too had this view. But now there were cracks in her window. And the light coming through those cracks had an unexpected quality to it. Part of her wanted to still believe as she always had that old superstitions were simply born out of ignorance. But another part of her longed to understand more, to find out what else she might have been wrong about.

"I'm not saying I know what to think," she admitted. "I'm just saying, something happened last night. Something real."

"Do you think that's what happened to you?" Evans asked. "You were possessed?"

She considered this. She had no frame of reference for how to answer that question. So she shrugged. "I don't know for sure."

"You travelled eighteen miles in less than twenty minutes," Evans said.

She looked at him, wondering what he might be suggesting with that observation. It was remotely possible she could have been thrown in a vehicle and driven there. But that vehicle would have to have been traveling at a very high speed, on mountain rounds in New Hampshire. It was not a straight shot. There were stops along the way, and sections of road that required a slower speed. Wilson had said there were speed traps. They would have been seen. It was a trip that should take any normal driver closer to thirty minutes.

"So how do you explain that?" Mitchell countered. "Aliens?"

Evans sighed. He shook his head.

"Look, I don't know how any of this works," she said. But Diego is right. These things, they say they want to help ... but everything they do is ..." She shook her head. "Besides, you said it yourself. The odds of us actually coming in contact with intelligent life from another planet are impossibly small. So, how did I travel those eighteen miles in twenty minutes?"

Evans looked off. Mitchell smiled, allowing a slightly bemused laugh escape from her lips.

"Maybe we both have some things to think through," she offered.

Evans looked back at her. He nodded again. "Can we go home now?" he asked. "I think I need to call my therapist."

Mitchell laughed. He smiled.

"Yeah," she said. "Let's go home."

They each moved to their respective sides of the car. Mitchell as usual got behind the wheel. She started the car and pulled out onto the road. Taking one last glance, she felt the pang of regret that she wasn't out there on that field. After everything, she couldn't help anymore. But she'd done what had to be done. That would have to be enough.

She stepped on the gas and they pulled away from the scene. As they began to pick up speed, a news van heading in the opposite direction passed them. Then another. They would be swarming the site soon. How the FBI would choose to explain how they had come upon such an important tip as to the location of Tommy Ferguson's body would certainly be interesting. She could see it tonight on the news. Maybe they'd call it an anonymous tip and hope no one asked further questions. Maybe she'd order a pizza and watch the news. Maybe she'd call her mother. Could she tell her what she had been through—what she was going through still? Mitchell had enough self-awareness to know that she'd slept like a rock last night thanks to how much she'd had to drink. But that was not a sustainable means of coping. How would she sleep tonight? Her skin still crawled as she recalled the exam table, the sound of the dark voice coming from Stephanie's mouth, the knowing hatred in her eyes. Something had definitely happened. She even dreaded the thought of being alone. But she'd have to be alone eventually.

No matter what she did next with the mundane things of life— job, living arrangement, moving or not moving cities, so forth—it was clear to her that her days of investigating were not exactly over yet.

The car headed downhill, picking up more speed. Mitchell squinted in the bright sunlight, enjoying how warm it felt on her skin. When was the last time she'd allowed herself to just enjoy the sunshine? It reminded her that not everything in this world was quite so dark and so cold.

AUTHOR'S NOTE

Socrates claimed that the unexamined life is not worth living, as quoted in Plato's *Apology*. Storytelling has always been and continues to be an essential way in which human beings examine life and make sense of our world. Today, neuroscience and evolutionary psychology confirm that we survive by creating narratives.

That's why I say...

A life without stories is not worth living.

This is why I'm a storyteller. And this is why I explore how stories help us discover meaning. Join my exploration and uncover how the stories you love aren't just entertaining you, they're helping you live a more meaningful life. Read my blog at www.mikelwisler.com.

Communicating Belief and Intellect

Doxa (v): Doxa (from ancient Greek "glory", "praise", "to appear", "to seem", "to think" and "to accept") is a Greek word meaning common belief or popular opinion.

-- A Greek-English Lexicon

Noûs (n): (in Greek philosophy) mind; intellect.

-- Random House Kernerman Webster's College Dictionary

Media (n): A substance that makes possible the transfer of energy from one location to another, especially through waves.

-- The American Heritage Science Dictionary

DoxaNoûs Media is a publishing company focusing on fiction and nonfiction in the areas of entertainment, business, politics, theology, and civil discourse.

Website: www.doxanousmedia.com

Facebook: @DoxaNousMedia

Twitter: @DoxaNousMedia